# RENEGADE STAR

J. N. Chaney

www.jnchaney.com

1st Edition

# BOOKS BY J.N. CHANEY

**The Variant Saga:**

The Amber Project

Transient Echoes

Hope Everlasting

The Vernal Memory

**Renegade Star Series:**

Renegade Star

Renegade Atlas

Renegade Moon

Renegade Lost

Renegade Fleet

Renegade Earth

Renegade Dawn

Renegade Children (Sept 2018)

**Standalone Books:**

Their Solitary Way

The Other Side of Nowhere

# CONTENTS

For Sarah -

how lucky that I should live

at this moment

on this planet

in this galaxy

and, despite the odds,

meet and love a girl like you.

# ONE

"I'LL FUCKING KILL YOU!" screamed William Emmerson as he ordered his security personnel to fire in my direction.

"Good luck with that!" I returned, running as fast as my feet would carry me.

I tore through the woods outside the Emmerson Estate, having just stolen an object worth two hundred thousand galactic credits—a small metal orb about the size of my fist.

A merchant named Fitz, one of Emmerson's rivals, hired me to deliver this junk for a reasonable price. I didn't really give a shit about their feud, but the pay was good and I needed the work.

"Stop him!" shouted Emmerson. "Someone stop that bastard!"

I could hear the dogs barking far behind me as I neared the clearing. If Emmerson thought a couple of mutts and some hired goons would be enough to slow me down, he had another thing coming.

"Excuse me, sir," said a voice in my ear. It was Sigmond, my ship's A.I. unit. "I see you're being chased. Shall I drop the cloak and prepare for departure?"

Another energy blast went flying by my head, throwing a

shower of splintered tree bark and oxidized sap into my face. I gripped my pistol and swung around, spotting the guard between branches and undergrowth. I waited for a clean shot, then squeezed the trigger and fired, sending the bullet straight into the man's leg, dropping him to the ground.

"That'd be great, Siggy," I said, breaking through the tree line and into the open field. "Try to make this quick, pal, unless you wanna be homeless."

"Perish the thought, sir."

*The Renegade Star* rippled as it phased into visibility right in the middle of the valley. Several more security personnel came running after me, emerging from the forest, setting their sights on me and firing.

I burst forward, shredding grass with the heel of my boot. Several shots fired in the distance, whizzing by so close they rang in my ear.

"Hurry!" shouted Emmerson, joining his rent-a-thugs. He continued with a garbled, unintelligible slew of insults.

Meant for me, I assumed.

I turned and aimed as I ran, shooting as accurately as one could expect, given the situation. This managed to startle the other men, forcing them to take cover.

Four dogs entered the field, racing after me, snapping their jaws as they ran. Within a few short seconds, they were already halfway across the glade.

"Get us out of here," I said as I finally reached the ship. "Raise the lift!"

The dogs were closing behind me. I could hear the anticipation of the kill in their labored breaths as they gained ground.

The cargo bay gate began to rise, and I leapt into it, sliding along the floor with my pistol trained out the narrowing airlock.

The animals tried to jump in after me but fell short. They leapt and snarled, showing their teeth as the half-closed gate continued to raise.

Several blasts struck the side of my ship. "Fuck you!" I heard Emmerson shout.

*The Renegade Star* lifted from the ground. I held the railing, watching through the closing cargo bay as nearly two dozen armed guards and their master aimed their rifles at me and fired.

More shots peppered our hull, but I knew we could take it. This ship was built to withstand a hit from a quad cannon, so a little handheld firepower wouldn't do much except scrape the paint.

As the airlock sealed and daylight was replaced by the cruising floods, we accelerated. For a brief moment, I felt the pressure, until the stabilizers kicked in and it was smooth sailing.

At about this time, we entered the stratosphere. From Emmerson's point of view, we were already gone.

I ran up the stairs and made my way to the cockpit, where I

took my seat and strapped in. On the dash, an old bobblehead of Foxy Stardust, a cartoon character, was still bouncing from the earlier turbulence. She had a white helmet with a neon blue visor and a pink spacesuit.

"Raising the cloak," said Sigmond, right as we entered the stratosphere.

No doubt, Emmerson was fuming over what I'd done, although it wouldn't matter soon. After I delivered this trinket to Fitz, all the blame would shift to him. If there was any revenge to be had, Fitz would bear the cost of it, not me. That was how it usually went for people in my line of work. We did the job, but the client was always the one who shouldered the blame.

My name is Jace Hughes and I was a Renegade. A hired gun. I'd been known to smuggle, steal, loot, and even kill, should the need arise, and I'd keep on doing it until I was dead.

It was the life I'd chosen, and I had no regrets.

* * *

"What the hell is this?" I asked, staring at the blinking red light on the dash.

"That would be the warning light, sir," remarked Sigmond.

"Since when do we have a warning light?" I asked. "And how do I make it stop?"

The light went dead as soon as I finished. "Apologies, sir. It seems our sudden arrival triggered it. The sensors were overwhelmed."

"Oh," I said, turning back toward the glass and the current battlefield. Over four hundred ships across two fleets were currently fighting it out, blasting themselves to pieces. I couldn't say why this was happening. That's not why I was here.

We were flying above Galdion, an isolated planet on the edge of the galaxy, having just broken through the thermosphere on our way out. I'd arrived in pursuit of an item of interest, dropped here specifically for me to pick up and deliver. Had I known I'd be leaving through a war-zone, I might have arrived at a later time.

"Do any of them see us?" I asked, referring to our cloaked vessel.

"Not yet," answered Sigmond.

"How soon can we jump?" I asked, bringing up the star map.

"Approximately forty-five seconds," responded Sigmond. "Longer if we die."

"Funny as always, Siggy." I punched in the coordinates for Taurus Station, our next destination and my current home of record.

"Thank you, sir," said the A.I. "I really do aim to please."

The ship jerked sideways, and I gripped my chair. "The hell!" I barked.

"Shields are holding," remarked Sigmond, an unimpressed tone in his voice. Normally, A.I.'s weren't outfitted with personalities, but I made it a point to request one when I had Siggy commissioned. If I was going to spend weeks at a time inside this ship, it wouldn't be with a monotone, talk-me-to-sleep artificial intelligence. "Neither side has spotted us yet, thankfully, and the cloak is holding. Both enemy shots were targeted at other ships."

Some distance from the planet, several Master Class Cruisers lay waiting. It would be difficult to leave this area without being spotted, even with the cloak. *The smaller fighters won't be able to detect us,* I thought. *But those Cruisers might.* "We'll have to show ourselves soon right before we make the slip. Think we'll have enough time?"

"I believe so, sir," said Sigmond. "Though, I may have to return fire, should they spot us."

"Let's try to avoid a firefight, Siggy. The last thing I need is another warrant."

"Perhaps next time you won't bring us to such a dangerous location," said Sigmond.

"I will if I want to eat," I told him. "Or would you rather we not get paid?"

"There must be easier lines of work," said Sigmond.

"Easier ain't always better, Siggy," I said with a grin. "I'll take the Renegades over sitting behind a desk any day of the week, thank you very much."

Another blast rocked the ship, this time from the rear, and the attacking vessel passed by overhead. It was a strike class Arnesian raider. "Are we ready yet?" I asked.

"Incoming slip in twelve seconds," said the A.I.

I watched the two fleets duke it out, with ships exploding across the battlefield like fireworks, leaving fields of floating debris in their wake. In a matter of hours, the entire orbit of this planet would fill with wreckage. Dozens of salvage crews were likely already standing by, eager to resell the parts to the open market, possibly to the very organizations involved in this fight. Ships would be rebuilt, pilots trained, and the cycle would continue. Before I joined the Renegades, I might've been there with them, waiting for my scraps.

Not anymore. Now I had a more active profession. Sure, it was dangerous, and I'd probably get myself killed before I turned fifty, but I'd rather die from a blaster than boredom.

"Dropping the cloak and initiating slip," announced Sigmond.

I gripped the manual controls for the quad cannons. "Let's do it."

The screen showed the cloak dropping, leaving us vulnerable to detection. "Readying slip," indicated Sigmond. "Six seconds until activation."

I nodded. "That should be quick enough to—"

Before I could finish, two Arnesian raiders broke formation, turning toward us. "We're being scanned," said Sigmond. "They are readying weapons."

I let out a quick sigh. "Can't say I didn't try."

I aimed the digital reticule at the first ship, squeezing the trigger once the computer had the lock. The quad cannon sprayed a series of rapid shots at the enemy vessel, punching a six-meter hole straight through its cockpit, obliterating the pilot and setting the ship to drift like a dead fish in a calm lake.

Immediately, I turned my attention to the second, firing another wave. To my surprise, one of the shots tore through the center of its hull, splitting it apart instantly and igniting its core. The propulsion engine reacted the only way it knew how—by exploding.

The ship shattered into countless pieces of unsalvageable dust, scattering towards the planet.

The rest of my shots continued, unabated, into the darkness of space. A few fell to the planet's surface, followed by the debris from the destroyed ships, most of which would disintegrate before it could touch the ground. My shots, however, would continue until they hit something. Part of me wondered if any of them would strike Emmerson's plantation, but I wouldn't stick around to find out.

I had shit to do.

"Initializing slip," said Sigmond, and suddenly the entire battlefield vanished.

I watched as we entered the slip tunnel, the buried dimension that doubles as an express lane. Most of slipspace was still largely unexplored, but at some point, we figured out how to use it to transport ourselves across vast distances. Traveling through it wasn't instantaneous, by any means, although it was certainly faster than using normal space. Instead of taking centuries to travel from one-star system to another, you only had to wait a few hours, maybe days or weeks, depending on how far apart the systems were.

Right now, I was looking at six standard hours, give or take a few minutes. That gave me time to nap and take a piss, maybe snag a sandwich. "Siggy, let me know before we're out. I need to be alert when we get there."

I leaned back in my chair, observing the passing lights along the slip tunnel. I had no idea what they were, and I didn't care to learn. I wasn't a scientist, and I liked the mystery.

I reached down beside my foot and touched the package, a metal orb, tightly secured. I'd risked my life to track down, retrieve, and deliver this thing.

Whatever it was, it must hold some kind of value, I wagered, but gods only knew if I'd ever find out. Scans had shown it to be safe, so it wasn't a bomb or anything dangerous.

In my time running jobs, I'd pulled a few heists for collectors, so I knew this crap sold well on the market. Fools like Emmerson paid millions to have them dug from the ground and placed in a dark room, giving artificial value to a meaningless trinket. If you asked me, it all came down to someone with too much money to spend, looking for more ways to spend it.

That was fine with me, because jobs like this kept me

employed.

Being a Renegade sometimes meant doing whatever job you could get, so long as it kept your ship in the sky. It meant shutting up and getting paid.

Outside of that, nothing else mattered.

# Two

"Ten thousand credits," said Fitz, pressing his thumb to the pad. "Now, give me the orb."

"Here you go," I said, tossing it to him.

He caught it with both his hands, right in the flab of his gut. I watched him marvel at it, studying the detailed designs engraved in the metal. "Marvelous."

"Glad you approve," I said.

"Oh, yes. This is great!" he smiled. "That shithead Emmerson must be so pissed right now. I hope he's ripping his hair out. Did you see his face when you took it? How angry was he?"

"It was hard to tell with all the gunfire."

"I bet he killed one of his men after you left. He does that sometimes," Fitz said, laughing.

"You got any other jobs for me?" I asked.

"More?" asked Fitz. "No, nothing else right now. Maybe in a few more weeks. Things are slow these days, you know?"

"Sure," I said.

"Why you asking? You feeling an itch in the old trigger finger?"

*Dammit. I could've used another job.* "I've got some debts I have to square."

"That's too bad," said Fitz, grinning. "You ought to make better life choices."

"Says the guy who hired me," I remarked, ignoring his sarcasm.

He gave me a cheeky smile. "Maybe so. Say, you wanna know what you stole?" He lifted the orb in front of me.

"Not particularly," I said.

He chuckled before tossing it behind him. "Well, it's nothing, really. I just heard it was Emmerson's favorite toy. He collects old shit and pretends it's treasure. He thinks it makes him sophisticated or something."

The orb rolled along the floor, stopping when it hit the base of his chair.

"Oh," I said.

"When he finds out I have it, he'll be so furious. I *hope* he tries to come after me. Did I tell you what he did to me?"

"He stole your territory," I said, hoping to avoid what he was about to tell me.

No such luck.

"He did more than that! I was the only dealer in X-92 fuel for three systems until he showed up. I had a monopoly on over thirty high-demand items. Emmerson comes around and starts undercutting me on every bid. Can you believe that? He's got no idea who he's messing with. I'm going to—"

I turned away and started to leave. "See ya later, Fitz. Good talking to you."

"W-Where are you going?"

"I've gotta be somewhere. Call me if you get another job."

He swallowed, recomposing himself with a large grin. "Maybe I'll have you steal the rest of his collection next time. I'll be in touch!"

"So long, Fitz," I said, leaving his foyer. *You crazy bastard.*

When I was outside, near my ship, I tapped the com in my ear. "Siggy, how's my money looking?"

"Ten thousand credits have been transferred from multiple shell accounts into yours," said Sigmond.

"What's my total after the transfer?" I asked.

"Ten thousand, forty-seven credits."

"Hold on a second. You mean I only had forty-seven credits in my account before this? Where'd the rest of it go?"

"Fuel and repair costs to the ship, as well as the new coffeemaker you installed."

I nodded. "All important things."

"Including the coffee?" asked Sigmond.

"*Especially* the coffee," I answered, imagining myself with a cup in my hand, breathing in the delicious aroma. "You don't have taste buds, Siggy, so I'm willing to let that one slide."

"You're so very kind, sir."

\* \* \*

As we left the planet, Sigmond informed me that we had a call. "From who?" I asked.

"Fratley Oxanos. He wants to speak with you about—"

"Money," I said, finishing the thought. "Put him through."

A second later, I heard several voices on the com, each one laughing and shouting. It sounded like a party. "Hello? Is that you, Jace?"

"I'm here, Fratley," I answered.

"Ah! You ornery boy. Tell me you've got my money."

"I'm working on it. I just did a job and now I'm on my way to collect on another."

I heard the crowd cheer, including Fratley. "Oh, did you see that? What a score! Sorry, Jace. I'm busy with a game. Did you say you had my money? Because that's the only answer I want to hear from you."

"I've still got two standard weeks left to pay you," I reminded him.

He laughed. "Aha! That's right, you do. How could I forget? I hope you're not waiting until the last minute, though. I'd hate to track you down."

"You'll have it, Fratley. Don't worry."

"That's what I like to hear, Jace! Now, leave me the fuck alone. I've got money on this game and I ain't losing."

The line clicked off. "Guess he hung up," I muttered.

"It would appear so," said Sigmond.

I leaned back in my seat, trying to relax. I owed that jackass one hundred thousand credits, which was far more than I had. I'd have to pull some serious jobs to get that kind of cash before the deadline. I might even have to sell my ship.

The thought sent a chill down my spine. Screw that. I'd let him cut my fingers off before I gave up *The Star*.

If only I hadn't taken out that loan, I wouldn't be in such a tight position.

I'd borrowed it from Fratley six months ago to pay for a cloaking device, which I believed would give me the edge I needed in this business to stay at the top. I was half-right about that.

Having a cloak helped more than I ever dreamed, but no matter how useful it might be, if the jobs weren't coming in, then what good was it?

A little while back, the Union government started cracking down on Renegades, making it even more difficult for clients to find us on the market. This happened from time to time, maybe once every other year, although it never lasted. We used a private network within the Galactic Net to maintain privacy. Sometimes the Union pups got lucky and broke through our security, and sometimes they'd make an arrest, but it was always tough to stick. None of us used names. Only codes.

Mine changed every two weeks.

Our guys managed to restore security within a day, although the damage was done. A large chunk of clients dropped contact, leaving me and every other Renegade without any work. They'd all come back, just like every other time this happened, but not for a few more weeks.

Until then, I was out here trying to grab whatever I could. Any job to get the credits so I could pay off what I owed. Fratley didn't like to give extensions, so I couldn't count on that. I'd have to find a way to pay the debt before time ran out.

Which was why I needed to check in with Ollie Trinidad, my own personal agent. If anyone had a job for me, it was going to be him.

* * *

I arrived at Taurus Station and ordered Siggy to mind *The Star* while I was out. "Anyone fucks with you, you know who to call."

"Station security?" he asked.

"No, you call me so I can shoot their asses. Security would only get in the way."

"Right, of course," said Sigmond.

I went straight for the bar, leaving my quarters for later. I wasn't tired or bored enough to call it a day. Not until I had some booze in me.

Percy's Bar was in the corner of the promenade, but it wasn't what you'd call fancy. If anything, I'd say it was a pile of shit, barely holding itself together.

"What can I get you?" asked the barkeep, a new guy I didn't recognize.

"Where's Mort?" I said, taking a seat.

"You didn't hear? Mort died a few weeks back. There was a memorial dinner here. We posted signs around the station."

"Damn," I muttered. "Sorry I missed it."

The man pulled out a bottle of gin and poured a cup. "Here you go, friend. This one's on the house."

I took the glass, never one to turn down a free drink. "Thanks, pal."

I stayed there a while, watching people pass through the promenade with shopping bags and busy conversations. There were only a handful of people in the bar itself, probably because it was only the middle of the afternoon.

"We've received a report regarding the attack on Senator Gibson," said a man's voice, catching my attention.

I turned to see the Union News Network on the view-screen. The anchor, whom I recognized as Quintin Dallas, was a clean-shaven reporter with brown hair in his mid-thirties. Like every other person on mainstream television, Quintin was nothing more than a mouthpiece for the Union government, spewing propaganda and bullshit at every turn.

I took a sip from my drink as I watched.

"It appears the assassin broke into a special research facility to attack and kill Senator Gibson, most likely because of his affiliation with the New Dawn political movement, which aims to crack down on border security along the Deadlands. The Deadlands, for those unfamiliar with the term, refers to the edge of Union-controlled space between the Osiris system and the Velos Nebula. We here at the UNN caution all Union citizens to please inform your local representative of any suspicious—"

The view-screen clicked off. "I hate that jackass," said the bartender. "Always with the lies. I only had it on this channel because of the game before this shit. You know, that senator he's talking about was corrupt. I heard he was the guy behind the bill that called for all those arrests a few months ago."

"Arrests?" I asked.

"The government went and seized a bunch of planets near the border. They arrested anyone with authority or any outstanding warrants. One of 'em was my brother-in-law. I heard he's working in a mining colony now. Those politicians ain't nothing but crooks, if you ask me."

I nodded my agreement, then drank the last of the alcohol, setting the cup back on the counter. I transferred my payment into his account as well as a nice tip. "Thanks for the drink," I said. "I'll see you next time I'm in."

"Stay safe, friend," he said as he wiped the counter with a dirty rag.

I waved my goodbye and headed out into the crowd on the

promenade, squeezing my way toward the other end. My next stop would be the parts department and the station fuel center, not to mention a visit to Ollie's place. All routine whenever I returned from a recent job. This was the part I hated most about being a Renegade.

Check-ins and paperwork, but maybe Ollie had something fun for me to do—another smuggling gig or something involving a break-in. Whatever the case, I was ready to hit the sky again.

# THREE

"Here you are, Jace," said Ollie, fanning a pad in my face. "Two thousand creds, the last of your payment from that job you pulled two weeks ago for Antonio Ariguellio."

I took the pad from his hand, examining the transaction. The funds had been sent directly into my account—one that wasn't tied to my real name, of course. "Good. Now I can finally afford to get a decent piece of meat on this station."

"You mean from Jarro's?" he asked, raising his brow. "Pretty sure they shut down."

My eyes widened. "What?"

"Yeah, heard the owner fell into some money problems. Borrowed from the wrong guys, you know?" He snickered. "Hey, probably from guys like me."

I cursed under my breath, handing him back the pad. "Don't kid yourself, Ollie. You're not that menacing."

I started to leave when he raised his finger. "Hang on, I've got another job."

"Oh?" I said, pausing.

"Two actually." He glanced at his pad. "Antonio again. He's

asking for you, specifically."

"What's it about?"

"Not sure you'll like it," he said, twisting his lips.

I could tell by his expression that he was probably right. Ollie knew me better than anyone, much as it pained me to admit. "Just tell me."

"Looks like his ex-wife took off on him, so he's putting a hit out. He's pretty sure she's in the Deadlands somewhere. Looks like she stole some money and ran off with her bodyguard. It pays thirty thousand creds."

"Doesn't she have a kid?" I asked.

He hesitated a second, then nodded. "That's in here, too. Antonio wants you to take out the boy. He—"

"Pass," I said without any hesitation. "You know I don't mess with kids, Ollie."

He nodded. "I know, but I had to tell you. It's my job."

"What else you got?"

"Only one more." He reached beneath the counter and brought up another pad. "It's an escort job. You'd be taking a woman to Arcadia."

"Isn't that the place with the priests?"

"The Church of the Homeworld, I think," said Ollie, trying to remember. "Yeah, that's them. This lady's got some cargo she needs delivered there."

I bent over the counter and looked the little man in the eye.

"You want me to take some nut back to her cult? What do I look like to you?"

He raised his hands. "Hey, I just give you the jobs, Jace. Don't blame me if you don't like 'em." He turned the pad around. I could tell the woman had an attractive face, although her clothes hid the rest. She wore one of those baggy gray tunics with a veil over her hair—standard stuff for a member of the Church, far as I could tell. I'd seen a few of these nuts on the news protesting the government, but who knew why. "Come on, Jace, what's a little girl like that gonna do? 'Sides, it seems like good money. Five thousand creds. Plus, she ain't bad on the eyes."

"Looks like a waste of time," I said, thumbing the pad away. "What else you got?"

He swiped the screen, frowning. "Uh, looks like nothing's come in yet."

"You only got the one?" I asked.

"It's been a slow week. What can I say?" He grinned, showing his crooked teeth.

I cursed again. "Fine, send it to me." I looked him in the eye. "She better not be any trouble."

"Hey, no promises. I just send you the jobs, remember?" he asked, still smiling.

"Sure," I said, grabbing the pad out of his hand. I tapped my thumb to the screen to accept the job. "Tell her to meet me at the ship tomorrow, and find me some better jobs while I'm gone."

"You got it, Jace. Anything for my best," he said.

Ollie owned a souvenir shop on the promenade that doubled as a Renegade Bounty Office (RBO). This entire station was a common stop for tourists making their way back from the Lenidas system, allowing Ollie to overcharge them for hastily-made trinkets. Everything in this store was absolute trash, but the vacationing executives with too much money were eager to buy them, probably to put on display for all of their spoiled friends.

The joke was on them, though. Half of this crap came straight out of the station's dumpsters, only to be cleaned and refitted with some wire and hot glue. Ollie loved the idea of his little garbage toys sitting on hundreds of mantles, like they were exotic art pieces. What a joke.

Despite all that, Ollie was still the only reliable RBO agent in six systems. I'd had disagreements with a fair share of them, but *never* him. He always shot straight with me, never tried to steal or do me wrong.

I wish I could say he did all that because of his ethics, but I think he just valued his life. He knew the second he tried to short me, I'd bury him.

I respected him for that, even if he was a crook who sold trash to rich people.

I left Ollie's little shop and grabbed lunch at a place called Sal's in the food court. Unsatisfied by the sorry excuse of a sandwich, I drank half a dozen beers and went back to my place—a living area about the size of most people's closet. It had enough room for a bed, a dresser, a small desk, and not much else. Not that I minded. My job kept me away most of the time.

Besides, when you own a big home, you get comfortable and don't want to leave. You get lazy and fat, watch too much entertainment, you get boring. No, to hell with that.

I'd take my ship and a job, thanks.

My room smelled like stale bread when I opened the door. I must have forgotten to clean up when I was here last time. No matter. I wouldn't be around for long.

I tapped my ear. "Siggy, you there?"

"Always, sir," said Sigmond.

"Looks like we have a new job tomorrow. It's an escort gig. Should be quick and simple. I'm sending you the coordinates now."

I entered the passcode for my ship's digital inbox and transferred the data.

"Received. Uploading now," said Sigmond. "When should I expect your return?"

My head was foggy from the booze, and I was dog-tired. No way I was getting up before 9AM. "Mid-morning," I answered. "Call me if I'm not awake by 10."

"I'll sound the alarms," said the A.I.

I tossed the pad on the dresser and sat on the bed, sinking into the tiny mattress. I'd have to leave tomorrow for this job. Escort some religious nut to her cult. Not the most exciting work for a Renegade, but simple enough.

* * *

I met Ollie at the airlock outside my ship. "Morning, Jace," he said with a joyful expression.

"Where's the nun? Let's get this over with," I said.

"Never the morning person, eh?" asked Ollie. "Don't worry, she's already inside the ship. Siggy's keeping her company."

I squeezed my hand, ready to knock some sense into him. "You let a stranger into my ship? What the fuck is wrong with you?"

He scratched his ear and gave an awkward smile. "I told her it was a bad idea. I even said you'd get pissed, but she told me the sooner she boarded, the quicker you could leave."

"I don't care if it takes us half a day to get off this godsdamn station, you don't ever let anyone on *The Star* without me being here. You got me, Ollie?"

"Yeah, yeah, I got you. Seriously, though, Jace, she's gorgeous. You gotta see." He raised his brow and gave me a knowing look.

"Ollie, I swear to gods." I walked past him and through the airlock.

"I'll see you when you get back!" Ollie called from behind me.

I glanced behind me as I walked. "See you later, pal."

"Good morning, sir," said Siggy, once I entered the inner

corridor.

"What's the status on our passenger? She in the lounge?"

"The cargo bay, actually," said Sigmond.

"What for?"

"Ms. Pryar wishes to remain in close proximity to her belongings."

"Pryar?" I said. "Was that her name?"

"Yes, sir. Did you read the report?"

"Sure, the sections that mattered. Her name wasn't part of the job."

"If you say so, sir. Shall I have her meet you on the bridge?"

"No," I said, passing by the lounge. "I want to see what she's carrying."

My ship wasn't huge, but it had enough space to house several people and a fair bit of cargo. Depending who you were and where you came from, *The Renegade Star* was either massive and beautiful or a flaming pile of floating garbage. Either way, I didn't care. My baby kept me alive and got the job done.

The walk from the airlock to the cargo bay was short, saying nothing as I entered the familiar space. The woman stood beside a large, plain-looking crate. "You must be the nun," I said, plainly.

She turned to look at me, wearing the same garments from the picture I'd seen in Ollie's shop. They still covered most of her body, keeping her hair out of sight.

However, what she did let people see was beautiful. Large,

brown eyes, a thin nose, and a fair complexion. It was a mix of natural beauty and proper grooming. I wondered, briefly, what she might look like in a normal outfit.

"You must be the thug," she mocked, turning her back to me. "Are we leaving? I'd like to depart as soon as possible."

"I got that impression when you barged into my ship."

"I didn't barge anywhere. Your employer let me in. Besides, would you rather I take my time or do you want to get this over with and get paid?"

I scoffed. "Did you just call Ollie my employer?"

"Isn't he?" she asked.

"That little runt doesn't employ anyone except himself. I'm a freelancer."

"Call yourself whatever you want. Now, can we get going?"

I glanced at the massive crate at her feet. It was about two meters long, half-a-meter wide. "What's in the box?"

"Supplies for my church," she answered, frankly.

"Care to open it?" I asked.

Her eyes widened. "Excuse me?"

"Something wrong?" I walked to the side of the crate. "I can't carry this unless I know what it is."

"That's not a possibility."

"Why the hell not?"

"There are perishables inside. If I break the seal, they'll ruin within a few days. The seal has to stay intact until I get home."

"So, food? That's what you're carrying?"

"Food and medicine," she explained. "Our congregation placed an order and I was sent to bring it back." She reached into her side pocket and withdrew a pad. "You can see the order form here."

I took the device and read it over. The document looked authentic, as far as I could tell. "Seems right," I said, handing it back. "Okay, go take a seat in the lounge while I get us clear of the dock."

"With all due respect, I'd rather wait here until we arrive."

"You want to stay in the cargo hold? What for?"

"I take my work quite seriously. I can't leave the church's supplies unattended."

I laughed. "You think someone's gonna steal your box? You realize it's just you and me on this ship, don't you? That box isn't going anywhere."

"Nevertheless, I'm staying with it."

"Fine, then you can find another ship," I said.

"Excuse me?"

"There aren't any seats in here, which means there's no safety harnesses. You go flying and bash your head, what am I supposed to do? I'd have to deal with a whole mess of paperwork, not to mention the mess you'd leave behind."

"I can't just—"

"You fly with me, you follow the rules. Stick your ass in the lounge or take your box and go. It's one or the other. No compromises."

She looked at the crate, clearly concerned. "I can't wait for another ship."

"Do what I say and you won't have to. That's the price of admission."

She paused. "Fine. I'll wait in the lounge, but only until we're clear of the station. That's acceptable, isn't it?"

"Whatever stirs your pot, lady. Spend the trip in this room all you want, just not when we're arriving or departing." I shook my head and turned to leave. "It seems like a lot of trouble just for a stupid box, if you ask me."

# FOUR

"We're away from Taurus Station, sir," informed Sigmond. "Setting course for Arcadia System."

"Good, now let's see about our passenger," I said, pulling up the security feed in the lounge. To my surprise, the nun was nowhere to be found.

"She's already on the move, heading back to the cargo bay," said Sigmond.

The display changed automatically to the woman's location. She was now standing firmly beside her crate, lording over it. "She's a loony one, isn't she?" I said, observing her.

"You did tell her she could return once we left the station. She stayed seated until we were clear."

"Whose side are you on?" I asked.

"Apologies," said the A.I.

Truth was, I didn't have a reason for ordering her to stay seated in the lounge, but whenever I had a new passenger, I made it a point to put my foot down right at the start. They had to know I was in charge, just in case something went south. Maybe the engines blew, maybe we ran into a nasty fight. Whatever the case, they needed to do as I said. Best way to make that happen was to enforce my authority early on.

Lucky for the nun, I didn't foresee any major snags. The trip was a straight shot from Taurus Station to Arcadia, less than sixteen Union standard hours. We'd be there within a day. A quick in-and-out job for me, which was perfect.

Once I made the drop, I'd call Ollie and see if any other jobs came in. If none had, I'd have to put in requests to every other agent I knew about, which wasn't something I did very often. If that failed, I'd have to figure something else out. *Let's hope it doesn't come to that,* I thought.

I watched the nun in the video as she stood, almost motionless, like a guardian statue beside her valued cargo. I was certain she was lying about its contents. I could see it on her face when she gave me that story. Whatever was in there, it wasn't just food and medical supplies. "Siggy, see if you can run a scan on our new friend's cargo."

"Proceeding. Just one moment."

I tapped my finger on the console. I'd never worked with any religious folks before. The only exposure I had with any church was when I was a homeless kid on Epsy. I remembered a priest named Shiggorath walking around the city, handing out pamphlets. He first ignored and then condemned me when I asked for some of his lunch, and that didn't sit right with me. After following him home, I waited for him to leave, then broke in and tried to steal whatever I could find. I was tossed in juvenile detention the next day.

After that, I didn't have to worry about food or clothes again for two years. They even taught me to read and write. Not a bad deal when I thought about it.

"Scan complete," said Sigmond, snapping me out of my thoughts. "No results."

I leaned forward in my seat. "What do you mean?"

"The box is lined with an ultrathin layer of Neutronium, preventing me from examining its cargo."

"Did you just say Neutronium?" I asked.

"Indeed, sir."

My mouth hung open as I sat there, staring at the nun and her box. Neutronium was an exceptionally rare type of metal, used primarily by the Union for both research and military purposes. Most scanners couldn't even tell the difference between it and normal steel, but every decent Renegade kept their records up to date, just in case something like this happened. You never knew what piece of information would come in handy on a mission.

Whoever this woman on my ship was, she certainly wasn't your average nun. Not if she had access to Neutronium, of all things.

"Do we have a way of getting through the metal?" I asked.

"There is no known method, according to my database. I could search the Galactic Net for more information, if you would prefer," said Sigmond.

"No, forget it," I said.

I sat there for a long moment, debating what to do. After a while, I stood and began to leave. "Siggy, standby to perform another scan, but wait for my signal. Use the earpiece, too." I tapped the side of my head. "Got it?"

"Of course," said the A.I., and I heard his voice in my ear this time.

"Time to go see what our passenger is trying to hide."

* * *

I entered the cargo bay and spotted Abigail next to her precious crate, standing quietly with her hands in front of her waist. "I see you couldn't wait to come back here," I asked, making my way down the stairs to the lower platform.

She turned, a surprised look on her face. "You said I could—"

"I know what I said. Sit with your box. Do what you want. Just stay away from my stuff, you got it?" I motioned at the stack of supplies in the back of the bay. "I've got a lot of important shit down here, you know."

I walked over to my personal locker, opening it and removing an old hat, which I proceeded to wear. "Looks good, right?"

"I assure you, I've no interest in your things," she said, turning away from me. She stood there a moment, then glanced down at the crate.

I returned the hat and shut the locker. Leaning against the nearby metal beam, I crossed my arms and eyed her brown and gray tunic. "You mind if I ask you a question?"

"What?" she said, clearly distracted.

I reached into my pocket and took out a piece of rock candy, then tossed it back. Everyone had a vice. Mine was rock candy, those little hard fruity-flavored candies they made for old people and kids. "I said, can I ask you a question, lady?"

"Oh," she said, finally understanding. "I suppose so."

"What's with the whole church thing?" I asked, sucking on the delicious cherry sweet.

"Excuse me?" she asked, almost offended.

"The church thing. Whatever *this* is about." I motioned at her entire outfit. "What's the story there?"

"I'm not sure I know what you mean. I'm a devout follower of the church. My mission is to serve the teachings of our order as best as I—"

"Yeah, I get all that," I said, waving my hand at her. "I'm asking, why? What makes someone go and join the church?" I bit down into the candy, breaking it. "Your church is in the middle of the Deadlands. I read about it last night. It's not even considered a real religion by most people. How did a girl like you get swept up in such a nutty organization?"

"Excuse me?" she said, her look shifting from one of confusion to offense. "What right do you have to ask me such questions?

You're nothing but a brigand."

"I certainly am," I said, laughing at the insult. "You know what? never mind. It's none of my business."

She looked at the crate again, saying nothing.

"Guess I'll leave you to it," I said, and started to leave. "Although, I do have one other question, if you can spare me a second."

She didn't bother to look at me. "What is it?"

I swallowed what remained of my candy. "What's a woman like you doing with Neutronium?"

She froze at the question, her fingers going stiff at the mention of the last word. She knew exactly what I was talking about, no doubt about it. She must understand how this looked.

"I'm waiting," I said.

She finally turned around. Her face was serious, more than it had been before. "I don't know what you mean."

I looked at the crate, then again at her. "Is that right?"

She nodded, slowly.

"Your box is lined with one of the rarest materials in the galaxy, but you don't know anything about it?"

"Even if I did," she said. "It's none of your business, sir."

"See, normally I might be inclined to agree with you," I said, taking a step to the right, moving closer to the box. "But right now, I'm thinking you lied to me when you boarded this ship. I'm thinking whatever's in that crate, it isn't food or medicine." I took another step. "I'm thinking it's something I should be aware of."

"What I told you was the truth. I bought this crate from a shop in Cretos. I had no idea—"

A light tapping sound filled the cargo hold, and I froze in place. It was very light, but also close.

"Is something wrong?" asked the nun.

I held up my finger to quiet her.

Tap. Tap. Tap.

Tap. Tap. Tap.

Abigail and I made eye contact right as my hand slid down to my holster. I held the butt of my pistol.

"What is that?" I muttered, looking down at the crate.

Tap. Tap. Tap.

The nun's eyes widened. "Nothing!"

"It doesn't sound like nothing," I said, stepping forward.

"Wait a second!" she insisted, holding out her hands.

"There's something inside that thing, isn't there?" I asked, drawing my gun, not aiming it.

"It's an animal," she blurted out.

"Is that right?" I asked.

"Please, leave it alone," begged Abigail. "You don't—"

I raised the gun, showing it to her. "Keep pushing me, lady. I swear, I won't think twice about spacing you *and* your weird box." I pushed the gun forward, motioning with the barrel. "Back up."

She did as I ordered, giving me room. "Please, don't do

anything rash!"

"You try anything and I might," I said. The crate had a locking mechanism on it with a touchpad. "What's the code?"

"Please, you can't open that. It's not—"

I tapped the side of my pistol. "I *said*, what's the code? Don't make me ask again."

"It's not that kind of lock," she said, nervously.

"Then, what kind is it?"

"You...need my thumbprint. I'm the only one who can do it."

I lowered the gun and motioned for her to get on with it.

She edged her way closer to me and the crate, bending down to look at the lock. "Oh, this is no good," she said. "There's something wrong with it."

"What are you talking about? Open the damn box," I said.

She threw a hand up in frustration. "I can't! Look for yourself."

I leaned in to see what she was pointing at. The screen looked exactly the same as before. "I don't see any—"

Before I could get the words out, a hand flew up and snagged my wrist, moving it to the side. At the same time, I felt a jab in my gut.

Abigail was so fast, I had little time to react. Spit flew from my mouth as the blow struck me, and I gasped.

With the nun on her feet and holding my wrist, I pressed forward, shoving my knee into her bulky tunic and hitting her in the chest. She took the hit like a beast, surprising me, and tried to go for my neck.

I used my one free hand to grab hers. We struggled with one another, hand-in-hand. "What kind of nun are you?" I balked. Using my weight, I pulled her to the floor, slamming the woman on her back. She didn't scream or cry, but kept those determined eyes locked on me.

"You're pretty tough," I said, pinning her.

"Let go!" she snapped.

"Not until you open the box," I said.

She tried to position her leg beneath me, but I used my knee to lock her down.

Just then, I heard a click from behind us, coming from the crate. I looked to see the lid cracking open, condesation rising from within.

That was when I felt the nun's hand slip free of mine and hit me straight in the cheek. My face went numb from the slap, and it jarred me for a moment.

"Get off me!" she demanded, and for whatever reason, I did.

She let go of my other wrist and scurried over to the crate, leaving me with a red face and sitting on my ass. I still had my pistol, though it wasn't raised.

Abigail opened the lid to the box, letting a cloud of steam rise into the air. I eased up to my feet and leaned forward, eyeing the contents of the cargo. To my shock, I saw a figure—a girl with white hair, pale skin, and blue eyes—breathing steadily. A thick tube stuck out of her mouth, running into the back of the box.

The nun eased the tube out of the girl's mouth and throat. The girl responded by coughing erratically. She had green slime dripping out of her nose—a residue from the tubes.

Abigail helped her sit up and began rubbing her back until she vomited the contents of her stomach. It was standard for cryo-sleep patients, although I had only seen it a handful of times. Cryo-sleep wasn't common, except in extreme medical situations.

"You wanna tell me just what the hell is going on?" I asked, still gripping my pistol. I wouldn't use it against a helpless kid, but holstering it would be stupid.

The nun didn't answer. She swept her finger through the girl's hair, pushing it behind her shoulder. With the sleeve of her tunic, she wiped the girl's mouth and nose. "There, there," she whispered.

The albino child shivered in the cold, her eyes half-asleep. She opened her mouth to say something, although it was so light I couldn't hear it.

"Did you hear what I said?" I asked. "Who *is* that? You'd better start talking, woman."

"Her name is Lex," said Abigail.

The girl licked her lips. "Did we make it?" she asked, her voice finally audible.

Abigail shook her head. "I'm sorry. Not yet."

"Why am I awake?"

The nun turned to me. "Can you get a blanket, please?"

"Not until you tell me just what the fuck is going on," I barked.

The fire in Abigail's eyes had dissipated, replaced by a gentleness I hadn't seen before. "Please," she begged again, nothing but concern in her voice.

I stood there, not certain what to do. I looked at the girl in front of me. She couldn't be more than ten years old. No matter what circumstances had brought her to be in this position, no matter how outrageous the story, the fact remained she was just a kid.

I went to the nearby locker and took out a blanket, then handed it to the nun. "Here."

She took the blanket and wrapped it around the half-naked child. "Thank you."

With my hand still on the pistol, I leaned against the back wall, observing the two of them.

The girl leaned into Abigail's chest as she wrapped the blanket around her side. As she did, I could see the outline of a marking—no, a series of blue shapes along her side. They looked like tattoos.

"You'd better start talking," I said.

"It's complicated," said Abigail. "And frankly, none of your business."

"You bring a frozen girl on my ship, it becomes my business."

She ignored me, and looked at Lex instead. "Sorry about this, but the lock broke. You'll have to stay awake until we get there."

"Will I be safe if I do?" asked the girl.

"I promise you will," said Abigail.

"Hold on a second," I said. "Don't go making any promises to a kid like that. I'm about ready to drop you both off at the nearest station I find. Hell, maybe I'll just go back to Taurus and dump you where I found you."

Abigail furrowed her brow at me. "What about our deal? The whole reason I hired you was because Renegades will do any job they're offered."

"I'm not sure where you get your info, lady, but every Renegade is different. There's jobs I'll take and there's jobs I won't."

"So, you won't help us?" she asked.

"Look, it isn't even that you lied going into this," I said. "I don't actually mind that part. I just wanted to make sure you weren't carrying a bomb or something." I motioned at the girl. "But you've got a kid stashed in a box. What am I supposed to think?"

"It's not like that," she insisted.

Lex coughed, looking up at me with an exhausted expression. "Please, don't be mean to Abby."

"Abby?" I said, glancing at the nun.

The two of them stared back at me. I could sense their desperation. The need to survive, to keep going. If I didn't get them home, they might not have a second chance.

The truth was, I'd already decided not to toss them, but they didn't have to know that. Let them worry for a few more seconds about what the heartless Renegade was about to do.

"Tell me everything," I said, holstering my pistol. "You do that and maybe I'll take you the rest of the way."

"It's complicated," said Abigail.

I scoffed. "A fighting nun smuggles a frozen girl on my ship and tells me it's complicated. Lady, how much worse can it get?"

# FIVE

A lot worse, it turned out.

"Repeat that for me, one more time," I said, trying to process what I had just heard. "Because it sounded like you said you had the Union after you."

"That's right," said Abigail.

"The Union," I repeated. "The largest and most expansive government in thirty-two systems. The one with the most advanced military fleet in known space. That Union?"

She nodded.

"What did you do to piss *them* off? Aren't you supposed to be a holy woman? Or maybe you're some kind of assassin with all those moves you threw down on me a minute ago."

Abigail got to her feet. "I'm a lot of things, Captain."

"That much is clear," I remarked.

I wanted to turn and walk away from her right then, and maybe I should have, but I also wanted to congratulate her. I was no fan of the Union, by any means. They made my job more difficult every month with all their bullshit regulations and new laws, constantly encroaching on Deadland space and other territories that were supposed to be outside their authority. Half the reason anyone lived in those sectors was to avoid their massive oversight, only they were always pushing things. Always threatening to come in and wipe us all out.

Being a Renegade, an outlaw, was never as hard as it was right now. Not when the universe's biggest dictatorship decided to tell people how to live their lives, even when they weren't a part of their empire. Some believed it wouldn't be long until those bastards consumed the whole of humanity under their unified reach. All the free men and women, all the Renegades and independent colonies, would end up being nothing more than Union slaves, probably in the next few years.

If that happened, I'd have to change my name and find a new career.

Maybe something in agriculture. I always liked farming.

"Look," she began to say, but stopped herself, looking at Lex. She paused before continuing. "Let's talk in the hall, please."

I shrugged. "Whatever you say, Your Holiness."

We walked into the hall and left the weird-looking albino kid alone in her box.

She'd be fine. Probably.

Once we were out of earshot, I leaned against the corridor and asked, "So, what's the story?"

"Before I tell you, it's important for you to understand the this may implicate you. Everything we're caught up in could come back on you, Mr. Hughes."

"Just get on with it," I said, unfazed.

"Fine. The short answer," began the nun, "is that a division inside the Union has been abducting children. They've stolen them from across known space, from dozens of Union worlds, even a few outer-rim colonies, and, I'm not certain how much you know about the government, but—"

"Enough to believe what you're saying is probably true," I said, not ashamed of the hate I had for the government. I'd spent time with Union officers on several occasions. Most of it involved me getting shot at. I had no love for any of them.

"Good," she answered. "Those people have been doing this for years. The tests they're using on those children are complicated, so I won't get into it, but trust me when I say that Lex is lucky to be alive."

"Okay, so how did you get involved with a kid like that?" I asked.

"Someone in the department reached out to my congregation. They told us about the children, specifically about Lex, and we intervened. With the help of our contact, we managed to smuggle her out of the compound. We've traveled twelve systems to get this far, and now we're almost there."

"Twelve systems? That's three weeks of slipspace. Did she stay in the box the entire time?"

"For most of it. We had to refill the cryogenic fuel a few days ago, so we stopped at Taurus Station. I rented a room until you took the contract."

"Worst mistake I've made this week," I said. "And that's saying something."

"I'm sorry to hear that."

"You're sorry? I started this trip with just one crazy nun and now I'm stuck looking after some kid. You should be paying me double, trying to sneak a stowaway aboard like that."

"Double? Are you serious?"

"You paid for one ticket, not two. How is it fair to let that kid ride for free? This isn't a charity."

I expected anger, some sort of outburst at the notion of more money.

Only her eyes were soft and easy now, less angry than before. She seemed to accept what I was saying, like it made sense to her, or maybe she just didn't care. "Take us the rest of the way and the church will pay the rest. How does that sound to you?"

"Like a smart move on your end," I said, picturing the ten thousand credits I'd have at the conclusion of this trip.

I didn't like manipulating a nun for extras creds, but with Fratley breathing down my neck, I didn't have much choice. He was pushing hard for payment and I was running out of time. If I had to be a little mean to get it done, then I'd do what I had to.

Ten thousand wouldn't cover much of the debt I owed, but it was certainly better than five.

"Does that mean you'll fulfill the agreement?" she asked.

"Don't worry, lady. I'll get you to where you need to go. You just worry about paying me that money. That's your *real* job. Getting those credits. You got that?"

"I do, Captain," she said, taking a step back into the cargo bay.

"Call me Jace," I told her.

She didn't say another word. She simply returned to the little girl in the box. The albino child with the porcelain hair and the blue tattoos, who looked like the most innocent thing in the galaxy.

* * *

I sat in the lounge, staring at the little girl and her guardian nun as they slurped on some expired soup from my pantry.

Neither seemed to speak much, and when they did it was usually a short whisper.

Maybe they didn't want me to hear anything or maybe they just weren't talkers. Either way was fine with me, I decided. I liked the awkward quiet moments. They reminded me we weren't friends.

They also kept me alert.

"Sir, may I have a moment of your time?" asked Sigmond, piercing my ear like a cawing bird in the early morning.

"Right now, Siggy?" I blurted out. "What is it?"

Both of the females looked at me. I had forgotten that Sigmond's voice was coming through my earpiece rather than the overhead speakers.

"Just a second," I told them. "Small alert from the system. No big deal."

Abigail's expression didn't change, but I could see her fingers pressing into the table. The sudden outburst of mine had made her tense. No real surprise when I considered who she was running from.

I leaned back in my seat, placing my arms behind my head, staring at her in the most obnoxiously relaxed way I could. "What's up, Siggy? Got something for me?"

"We're reaching our first S.G. Point," said the A.I. "Shall I prepare to raise the cloak?"

"Sure. Can't be too careful," I said.

Abigail kept her eyes on mine. "Is everything all right?"

"We're about to hit a S.G. Point, so I was confirming with the ship's A.I. Don't worry about it."

"S.G. Point?" asked the girl, her eyes perking up.

I felt a pain in my stomach. I was so hungry. When was the last time I ate? This morning? "Siggy, do we have any of that Artesian bread left over?"

"I'm afraid not, sir."

"Damn it. I could've sworn we did. What am I supposed to eat? More soup?"

"What's an S.G. Point?" Lex said again, apparently not satisfied.

"It's where the ship comes out of slipspace," explained Abigail. "Only for a moment, though. Don't worry."

"Actually, that's only part of it," I said, only because I wanted to make the nun feel stupid.

"She doesn't need the full definition," said Abigail, giving me a look.

I ignored her, naturally. "It's called a Slip Gap Point. You know what slipspace is, kid?"

The girl nodded.

"Well, we use those tunnels to get around, but sometimes on long trips you have to leave one to enter another. It's like short pitstop. You follow?"

"I think so," said Lex.

"Right, so we just need to go back into normal space for a minute or three, then we'll launch into another slip. No big deal."

"Why can't we use the same tunnel until we get there?" asked Lex.

"Because not all of them go to the same place," I said.

"Oh! Are they like roads?"

I nodded. "Sure, kid." I took a drink of my beer, then looked at Abigail. "Better not be any Union ships when we come out, either."

"I wouldn't expect any. We've been exceptionally careful."

"Not enough," I said, taking another gulp of alcohol. "I found you out, didn't I?"

"You were lucky."

"Or you were sloppy," I said, forming the shape of a gun with my finger. I aimed at her and pretended to fire. "Either way, it doesn't matter. All that really matters is that it happened. You were found out."

"What's your point?" she asked, staring at my finger.

"That anything can happen, Ms. Pryar. None of us are ever safe."

* * *

The space between Taurus Station and Arcadia was riddled with all manner of unsavory sorts. That included pirates, smugglers, ravagers, and anyone else trying to avoid the eye of the Union. In other words, people like myself. I knew this stretch of space better than most, so I was aware enough to avoid staying in one spot for too long.

Countless jobs had me flying through this cluster of systems, which meant I had to be prepared for a multitude of dangerous possibilities. That was why I had the cloak installed in the first place, despite the costly overhead. I paid double the price of my actual ship for this thing, but it had saved my skin more times than I could count. At this point, I wasn't sure what I'd do without it.

We arrived out of the slip tunnel and back into normal space before long. "Initiating cloak," announced Sigmond.

I sat in the cockpit with the tracker on, checking to see who was around. The display showed a handful of ships positioned a short distance from us. This was not uncommon, since S.G. Points were often used as rest areas with traveling merchants setting up temporary shops to sell their goods. Unfortunately for us, I could already see this was not the case.

"I'm reading three ships," I said, examining the tracker.

"It appears they are ravagers," said Sigmond. "Amber class."

"So, small ones," I responded.

"Shall I fire a warning shot?"

"Is the cloak up?" I asked.

"It is," said Sigmond.

"Then, wait," I said. "They should know better than to mess with a cloaked ship."

"I believe you give people too much credit, sir."

I was about to tell Siggy he was wrong when one of the ships fired blindly at our position. I watched as the shot missed us and faded into the darkness of space. A quick glance at the tracker showed all three ships continuing toward us. "Here we go," I said.

"The enemy is using a hyperion shield generator. Be warned that our cannons will be ineffective at long-range."

"Great," I said, grabbing the controls. Hyperion shield generators were a massive pain in the ass because they could encompass an entire squad of ships, shielding all of them at once. We would have to pinpoint which of the three had the generator onboard and then get in close enough to perform an accurate strike.

I activated *The Renegade Star's* thrusters briefly, giving us some momentum before I cut throttle. *The Star* drifted forward, through the enemy formation as they continued firing blindly at the place we'd just left.

"Your orders, sir?" asked Sigmond.

"Wait until we're inside their shield. Once we're close enough, hit the one with the generator with the quad cannons."

"Understood," said Sigmond. "Entering enemy shield space in four seconds."

"Don't miss," I muttered. "And as soon as we down them, open a tunnel and move. You hear me, Siggy?"

"I hear you, sir."

I waited for the red light on my dash to turn green, indicating that we were close enough. I moved us behind the ship so that we were facing their exhaust. It was the weakest section of a ravager ship, by far, and it would give us the best chance.

The yellow light for the cannons came on, showing they were primed. "Preparing to fire," Sigmond said.

"Do it."

My seat vibrated as a series of missiles left *The Renegade Star's* cannons and struck the ravager vessel, ripping it apart. The ship exploded, sending chunks of debris forward into the void, a large piece of which nearly hit one of the others in the nose. The remaining two began to turn, and as they did, I fired again, directly through the field of debris, hitting several pieces of the destroyed ship, but also managing to strike the second in the wing.

He came forward, activating his thrusters, attempting to maneuver through his deceased comrade's remains. He must have figured that the debris would give him cover, but the same was true for me.

I released a mine, then activated my cloak and moved away from my current position, dropping thrusters as soon as I was able. The enemy ship approached my last position as it left the debris field, unaware of my actions.

As the ship activated its thrusters again, the mine attached itself to the ravager's hull, latching on and activating.

The explosion split the ship into three pieces, keeping the forward section intact. The pilot might actually survive this encounter, if he was lucky enough to be rescued.

But I wouldn't be the one to do it.

Before I could set my sights on the third ship, a shot came at me, grazing the side of my shield. Nothing to be concerned about. I responded with two of my own. The first hit the ravager in the upper hull, doing little damage, but the second managed to blast his weapons system, leaving him defenseless.

"Enemy ships disabled," said Sigmond.

I was able to fire again when the vessel turned toward the tunnel and performed a slip, disappearing and leaving me behind.

"There he goes," I muttered.

"Shall I pursue?" asked Sigmond.

"No, let him go," I said. "He's done."

There was a bang on the cockpit door. "Mr. Hughes!" came a muffled voice from the other side. "What's going on out there?"

"Quiet down, nun," I said, ignoring the question.

"It sounded like we were hit by something. Are we under attack?"

I went and opened the door to find the woman standing with her arms crossed. "A few ravagers tried to ambush us when we came out of slipspace," I told her. "I took care of it. Relax."

"Took care of it?" she repeated. "You mean you killed them."

"That's one way to put it, sure," I said, tapping my chin. "Another would be that I saved your life."

"Or nearly got us killed," she said.

"Either way, we're still alive, and ain't that what matters?" I asked, giving her a smirk. I turned my head, glancing back to the front of the cockpit. "Siggy? You ready?"

"And waiting, sir," he responded.

"Let's hit it."

I felt the ship rattle and, together with Abigail, I watched as a swirling blue light formed outside the cockpit window, expanding as we began to move into it. In a few seconds, we were inside, riding the currents of the slip, moving toward our final destination.

# SIX

We arrived in the Arcadia system, almost on time. To my surprise, the ravager ambush hadn't actually slowed us down that much.

When we came out of slipspace, I could sense the relief on Abigail's face. Her mission, as she saw it, was nearly at its end. I knew the feeling well, having performed so many jobs of my own, crossing borders with smuggled cargo, stealing precious items of interest from rich guys like Emmerson, and even ferrying crazy nuns from one corner of the galaxy to another. I always got that feeling of satisfaction when the goal was in view. I never fully let myself relax, because that would be shortsighted and stupid, but having most of the job behind me was always a good feeling. For Abigail, in this moment, she had to feel like all her efforts had been worth it. All the bullshit she had to go through was finally justified.

As we neared the planet, a representative of the church hailed me. "Incoming vessel, please identify yourself."

"You first," I said, deciding I wanted to be an asshole to this guy for no reason.

"This is Deacon Castiel. I am with the Church of the Home—"

"Thanks. I'm just here to drop off your nun," I said.

"To whom are you referring, sir?" asked Castiel.

"You know, the one who stole the little girl from the government and stuffed her in a freezer. Sound familiar? I hope it does or I might have to turn back around."

There was a short pause on the com before Castiel responded. "Y-Yes, sir! I'm so sorry. Please land at the following coordinates."

"Why, thank you," I said, tapping the bobblehead on my dash and watching its white helmet bounce.

"Shall I inform the passengers of our arrival?" asked Sigmond.

"Might as well. Make sure you remind the nun she has to pay me," I said, but paused. "Actually, I'll tell her. Think you can handle landing *The Star*?"

"Don't I always?" he asked.

I left the cockpit and went straight to the lounge. I found Abigail sitting on the side of a padded bench seat, with the girl on the floor in front of her. It looked like she was doing something to her hair. "Hey, both of you," I said, grabbing their attention. "It's time to go."

"We've arrived?" asked Abigail.

"Sigmond's bringing us down. Make sure you're ready when the doors open."

Lex turned and looked at Abigail. "Are we really there?"

"It seems so," said the nun.

"Finally!" exclaimed the girl. She sprang to her feet, bursting with sudden energy, a look of excitement in her eyes.

"Save that for when you're off the ship, kid," I said.

"We'll be ready soon," said Abigail.

"Good, and don't forget to have my money ready," I said.

"You'll have your payment, Mr. Hughes," said the woman. "I can promise you that."

* * *

I was surprised when I saw the church's landing bay. For being a religious organization out in the middle of nowhere, they certainly had some decent infrastructure. The design looked professionally built, but dated. Several decades old, I guessed, maybe more. This sort of setup wasn't uncommon for docking stations this far out. It was hard to find contractors outside of Union space. When you did, they generally overcharged for services.

"Please follow me," said a grown man in a silly outfit. Some sort of priest, I imagined. His clothes were similar to Abigail's but less elegant. Jewels hung from around his neck like he wanted me to know he was something special.

"Where to?" I asked, glancing back at Abigail, who was dragging her suitcase and having a hard time of it.

"The council will want to speak with you," said the man leading us.

"What about you?" I asked the nun, ignoring the escort.

"Lex and I have to go and meet with them first, separately," she said, frustrated by her luggage. She stopped and finally picked the bag up and carried it with both arms.

I didn't bother asking why the Council wanted to meet with us separately, because I already knew. In the event that I was dangerous or couldn't be trusted, they couldn't have me there, not until they fully debriefed the nun. "Whatever works," I said, then looked at the robed individual in front of me. "What else can you tell me about this Council, buddy?"

"The Council oversees all church matters, including those involving outsiders. You will need to meet with them to discuss your payment as well as any other matters they wish to cover."

"I don't have time for an inquisition. Just give me my money and I'll be on my way."

"If you want your payment, you'll need to see them," he said.

Lex ran up beside Abigail. "Can I stay with Mr. Hughes?"

"I'm sorry, Lex, but we have to go on our own for now. Besides, I'm certain Captain Hughes would rather handle things himself."

"You're not wrong," I said.

Lex frowned. "Mr. Hughes is more fun than priests."

I looked back at her. "You ain't wrong about that one either, kid. These weirdos wouldn't know fun if it bit them in the ass."

Abigail and Lex took a separate corridor as we entered the facility. I, however, continued to follow the man in the dress. He led me to a large hall with thick pillars, like something from an old painting. I didn't spend much time in holy places, so the whole sight made me uncomfortable. Maybe it was my hedonistic tendencies, because I couldn't shake the feeling I didn't belong here.

"Right this way," said the escort as he opened a massive set of wooden doors. "The Council will arrive within the hour. Please wait here until the appointed time."

"You expect me to sit around for an hour?"

He gave me a look that said he was growing irritated with me, then shut the door, leaving me alone. My thumb brushed the butt of my pistol. I didn't like being trapped.

The room itself was circular, not a single corner on the walls, and the furniture was sparse, with only a few seats and two tables along the back half. I sat behind one of them, already bored, throwing my feet up and leaning back.

In seconds, I felt the weight of sleep pulling me down. I didn't fight it, and instead let myself drift. If I was going to sit in this room with nothing to do, I might as well catch up on some sleep.

* * *

I opened my eyes to the sound of a door opening, scanning the room for intruders and clutching my pistol.

Several people entered through a secondary door, each with brown and silver robes. I watched as they walked to the rear table and took their seats, each of them staring at me.

"Hey," I said, waving slightly, my feet still on the nearby table.

"Thank you for coming," said the centermost councilmember, a woman with gray hair. She looked to be in her late seventies, if I had to guess. "My name is Sister Loralin."

I put my feet back on the floor, feeling pins and needles as the blood returned to my toes. "Nice to meet you," I said, unenthusiastically. "The guy outside said you wanted to speak with me about my money."

"That's right," she said, glancing at the other four people beside her. "We'd like to thank you for helping to deliver our cargo. We heard you ran into some trouble along the way."

"By cargo, I assume you mean the kid, but yeah, we hit a snag with some ravagers. My ship took some heavy damage, so I hope I get paid what I'm due."

"Sister Abigail informed us of your agreement. Rest assured you will be properly compensated." Loralin raised her hand, showing me a small pad. "As you said, you encountered some trouble, so we will raise your payment. How does fifteen thousand credits sound?"

"Fair," I said.

She tapped the screen. "The funds have now been transferred to your account, as promised. You have done us a great service and we appreciate it."

I pulled out my own device and checked my account. Sure enough, I now had an extra fifteen thousand credits. "Fantastic."

"Now that we've concluded that exchange, I hope you're willing to listen to another proposition."

"Huh?" I looked up at her. "What kind of proposition? You have another job?"

"We do, indeed," said a second councilman. He wore a large set of glasses and had graying red hair.

"What's it pay?" I asked, cutting straight to it.

Sister Loralin looked at her associates. "Double the previous one."

"Thirty thousand?" I asked. I hadn't had a job that paid so well in months. "What did you have in mind?"

"We need a capable pilot with a defensive ship," said the woman. "Someone to protect our vessel, should the journey prove hazardous."

"Where exactly are you trying to go?" I asked.

She hesitated to answer.

"I can't help if you don't tell me."

"Epsilon," Loralin finally answered.

I recognized the name immediately. The Epsilon system was one of the most dangerous in the Deadlands. You had to travel through a whole mess of problems just to get there. "You realize that system is in ravager territory, right?"

"Which is why we're asking you to help us," she said.

I considered the proposition for a moment. "How many people are you involving here?"

"Excuse me?" asked Loralin.

"What's the headcount on this trip? Are you sending a dozen people? Twenty? Fifty? Give me a number."

"That is undecided," said the man with the glasses.

"Okay, how about a rough estimate?"

"Possibly fifteen to twenty, but the number could increase," he answered.

"Think you could drop that to four or five?"

"For what purpose?" he asked.

"Just answer the question. Can you do it or not?"

The man glanced at Loralin, who gave him a slight nod. "We could if the situation called for such a thing, I suppose."

"Good, because that's almost certainly the only way you'll be able to make this nonsense work."

"What do you mean?" asked Loralin.

"You're not taking your own ship. We'll be using mine and nothing else, and I don't have room enough for all those people."

The man with the glasses scoffed. "Why would we only use one ship?"

"You don't have a cloak," I said, matter-of-factly. "I do, and it's the only way to move freely through ravager territory without being spotted. You take anything else in there and you'll be asking for trouble."

Loralin's eyes widened. "Your vessel has the ability to cloak itself?"

"It does indeed," I said.

The man gave me a curious expression. "Where did you acquire it? I thought only the Union had access to cloaks."

He was right. The Union spent more money on defense than any other governing body in the galaxy. The only reason I managed to find a cloaking device was because I borrowed a small fortune from a thug.

"Doesn't matter where I got it," I told them. "What matters is I've got one and you need it. Drop your crew size and I'll take them on my ship. I'll get you to where you want to go."

The councilors leaned in and whispered among themselves. After a brief exchange, Loralin cleared her throat and returned her eyes to mine. "Are you certain there is no other way?"

"Not unless you wanna get yourselves blown to pieces," I said.

"In that case, we agree to your conditions," she said. "We will begin preparations first thing tomorrow morning. We will also pay you thirty thousand credits—"

"A hundred thousand," I said, interrupting her.

She paused, but didn't flinch. "One hundred thousand?"

"I'm risking my life in the most dangerous section of the Deadlands and you only want to pay me thirty thousand? Don't think I can't sense when I'm being short-changed. You know you've got the money." I motioned around the room. "Look at this place. Don't act like you can't afford it."

"Very well," she said, agreeing to the new terms without

consulting her friends. "One hundred thousand credits."

Her sudden agreement threw me. I'd expected a negotiation of some kind, and she hadn't even tried to bring me down on the price.

I cursed myself for not asking for more. *Oh well,* I told myself. *Doesn't matter.* With the money I made from this job, I'd be able to pay off Fratley. That was the main takeaway here. That deadline was fast approaching and I couldn't afford to be choosy. "Fine, it's a deal," I told the old woman and her friends. "One hundred thousand credits for safe passage to the Epsilon system. There and back." I turned and started to leave. As soon as I touched the door handle, I felt it open from the other side. It was the same robed man from before. Before I continued, I turned back toward the Council one last time. "What's the mission for, by the way?"

"It's scientific in nature. We are interested in exploring a set of ruins," explained Loralin.

"Ruins?" I asked. "What in the gods' names for?"

"We believe they hold significant spiritual value. Nothing more or less."

"Whatever you say, lady," I muttered, turning back to the door.

With that, I was gone, headed back toward *The Star.*

\* \* \*

I sat inside the lounge, staring through the window at the

lands beyond the church's estate. The docking platform where my ship stood overlooked a wide valley, stretching nearly into the horizon. Surrounding it was a forest, dotted by a few small ponds and cut by a clear, flowing river. I debated taking the detachable shuttle and flying down there for a few hours, maybe get some fresh air for once.

I couldn't leave my ship unguarded, though, not in a foreign place like this, surrounded by strangers with an unknown agenda.

I didn't trust any of these people. It wasn't that I had anything against religious folks, but I knew practically nothing about them. It didn't help that they lived in such isolation. The only folks who did usually had something to hide.

Something big, too.

Whatever their reason was, I wouldn't feel at ease until I figured it out.

The sun fell below the horizon, sinking into the unknown like a falling rock in the sea. I watched as the blue sky turned black and filled with stars.

As the night went on, all the people disappeared into their homes. I left the lounge and made my way outside, climbing on top of the ship and resting my head against the hard metal hull.

I watched Arcadia's twin moons rise high above me, lighting up the night, joining thousands of stars.

I extended my arm and finger, connecting the lights, forming new constellations. It was something I did when I traveled to new worlds, if the situation allowed for it.

I formed a ship with my finger, its shape not unlike *The Renegade Star*. I found a woman's face, whom I named Julia, after my mother. She gave me pause as I stared into her eyes, and it brought me back to when I was young.

As I began to drift, my mind swirling with the fog of sleep, I spotted the outline of a man walking toward the distant night. I could almost hear Julia's voice, shouting at him to stay. *Where are you going?* she seemed to ask. *Why do you have to leave?*

# SEVEN

I dreamed I was in a field, standing with a plow, wearing loose-hanging clothes under a warm sun. The season had been plentiful, and the farm would do well this year. I had a wife with a pretty face and two children I loved very much. A strong boy and a beautiful girl. Both were in the field with me, helping their father, doing their chores.

We finished our tasks, tired from our work, and headed indoors to sit around the family table. I tore into a piece of bread and drank a glass of wine while my family laughed and teased each other. As the sun began to set, I thought this was a fine life and I was glad to have it. I wondered how I could ever want anything more.

And then I woke up, shivering in the cold wind of the early dawn. I looked at the hangar, momentarily confused about where I was and how I had come to be here. Why wasn't I in my bunk? And what kind of building was this? Why did it look so archaic?

The memories returned within moments, flooding back to me, replacing dreams with reality. I recalled being at Taurus Station and receiving the job from Ollie, meeting Abigail Pryar in the cargo bay of my ship, and discovering the frozen little girl in the box. I remembered getting into a scrape at one of the S.G. Points, and how one of them had gotten away. Finally, landing on this planet, and falling asleep on the top of my ship, under this foreign sky. It all returned to me in a heartbeat, but for that brief second, between being asleep and awake, I was somewhere else.

The haze of waking faded quickly, and before I knew it, I was myself again.

It was in that moment where people were their most vulnerable, the few seconds when they weren't entirely certain of who they were or what was going on. I hated everything about it.

"Did you sleep well, sir?" asked Sigmond, talking into my ear.

I groaned, feeling the discomfort along my spine from sleeping on a piece of hard metal. "Put on some coffee for me, would you, Siggy?"

"I shall begin the process right away."

I grabbed a change of clothes and a cup of liquid caffeine, then made my way to the front of the loading dock beneath my ship.

It didn't take long for the platform area to fill with activity. Two ships sat not far from mine, and I watched as several engineers began making repairs.

Far as I could tell, *The Star* outclassed every craft on this rock in terms of firepower. The ships were Stellar-class, which meant they could certainly move. Out here in the Deadlands, you either put your money into weapons or raw speed. If you could afford both, all the better.

Me, personally, I'd stuck a small fortune into my ship, which had saved my ass more times than I could count. Every credit had been worth it.

The door to the inner hall opened and out walked Abigail and Lex. The little girl smiled as she saw me standing on the loading dock, sipping my coffee and scratching my stomach.

"Morning, Mr. Hughes," said Lex, waving as she approached.

Both of them were dressed far more casually than before, especially Abigail. No church tunic on her this time. Instead, she wore a standard Union-style shirt and pants, the clothes of a working woman. I could finally see how fit she was, toned arms and a lean waist. No wonder she nearly put me on my ass the other day. Lex, meanwhile, wore a colorful shirt with a cartoon character on it.

"Welcome back," I told them. "I didn't know you were coming."

Abigail gave me a confused look. "Of course we are. Didn't they tell you?"

"All I know is I'm taking some priests to Epsilon."

"No priests, Captain. You're escorting the two of us and three academics." She paused. "Well, two are archaeologists. The third is a scholar."

"You look different," I told her, changing the subject.

"The situation calls for something different."

"What was the excuse before?"

"People ask fewer questions to members of the church," she said. "But as you saw, those clothes make combat difficult. We have no idea what we'll face in the Deadlands. I need to be prepared."

"You're not a normal nun, are you?" I asked, scanning her.

"Still a nun, though," she said, walking past me.

Lex ran up beside me, a wide grin on her face. "Mr. Hughes, can I go play with Sigmond?"

"Sure, kid," I said. "Go kick his ass."

She clapped her hands and ran up the platform and into the ship. "Sigmond, are you there?" I heard her say.

Right then, one of the nearby doors opened and two individuals walked into the hangar—a man and a woman. They made eye contact with me and proceeded forward, nodding in my direction.

"Sir," greeted a heavyset man with glasses and thinning blond hair. He looked nothing like the other priests. "My name is Dr. Thadius Hitchens. I'm the resident archaeologist. Pleased to meet you."

"Hitchens?" I echoed.

"That's correct," he said. "And this is my associate, Octavia Brie. We're to accompany you and Sister Pryar on your voyage. I promise, you won't even know we're here." He snickered. "Not until we've landed, that is. I doubt we'll be able to contain our excitement once we reach the dig site."

"The what?" I asked.

"The excavation site," said Hitchens. "Did no one inform you of the details regarding our trip?"

"All I know is I'm taking you to Epsilon," I said.

"That you are, sir," said the fat man. "But there's so much more to it. Have they really not bothered to fill you in?"

"Look, why don't you get on the ship and stow your gear. You can bore me to tears later once we're on our way."

"Right, of course," said Hitchens. "Come, Octavia. Let's do as the good captain asks."

Octavia nodded, and the two archeologists proceeded into the cargo bay.

I started following, but stopped at the sound of another door closing. I looked to see a young man running toward me. Unlike everyone else, he was actually wearing his priesthood robes. The only difference was his age. He couldn't be more than twenty years old. "Wait! Don't leave!"

I stopped and crossed my arms. "Now, what?"

"I'm so sorry!" said the young man, running with bags in his hands.

"Who the hell are you supposed to be? Father preschool?"

"Brother Fred...Frederick...Tabernacle..." he said, gasping and out of breath. "Sorry to...keep you, sir!"

"You didn't keep me. I was just gonna leave you behind," I

said.

"I'm so glad I caught you, then," he said, dropping his bags.

"You're just lucky you ran, Freddie. Two more minutes and I'd be gone."

\* \* \*

*The Renegade Star* lifted off the church's landing bay and began its ascent into the cloudy, vanilla sky. I asked Siggy to inform the passengers to stay in their cabins for at least an hour. We'd be out of the atmosphere long before then, but they didn't have to know that.

We breached orbit in less than fifteen minutes, entering slipspace shortly thereafter. We'd have to switch tunnels at least seven times before we arrived in the Epsilon system. If all went well, there wouldn't be a problem.

I left the cockpit and grabbed a quick bite from the food locker before any of the holy folks left their rooms. Soup and bread in my favorite chair.

"Can I have some?" I heard a sudden voice ask.

I looked to see Lex standing at the open doorway, staring at me as I sat with my food. "What are you doing out of your room?" I asked her.

She squirmed, and then shrugged. "I smelled it and got hungry."

"So?" I asked.

She frowned, her eyes fixated on my bowl. "Um."

"Fine," I said, pushing the bowl across the table, next to one of the other seats. "I've got more."

She smiled and ran to the table, giggling at the sight of the food. I got up and made some more, then joined her. "Thank you!" she said.

"Just eat," I said, dipping a piece of bread into the steaming soup.

She watched as I let the bread soak for a second, then tried to emulate my actions. I withdrew the bread and blew on it. She did the same, and then took a bite. Her eyes lit up at the taste. "Mm!"

"It's Tomato," I explained. "Expensive stuff, so you better not complain or—"

"So good," she said, taking another bite.

I watched her inhale the food. "Damn, kid. Didn't that cult feed you?"

She tried to answer, unable to get the words out with so much food in her mouth. Once she swallowed, she gasped. "Yeah, but it wasn't good," she finally said.

"What did they have?"

"Dumb stuff. It tasted like dirt," she said.

I nodded, then took another bite of my own food. We sat there together, eating soup and saying very little. The blue tattoo on her neck stuck out when she bent to dip another piece of bread in the bowl. I couldn't help but stare curiously at it. What kind of idiot had tattooed such a little girl? The nerve of some people.

"I don't know what it is," she said, suddenly. The words jarred me.

"Huh?" I blinked at her, and she stared back at me.

She pointed to the mark. "You want to know about it, right? Everyone always asks. That's why I was in the other place, before Abby found me. Those people wanted to know about it, too."

"It's a tattoo, isn't it?" I asked.

She nodded. "That's what *they* called it. The doctors from before."

"Doctors?" I asked.

"They were bad, but Abby stopped them," she said, taking another bite. "I never want to go back."

"Where did your tattoo come from?"

She shook her head. "I don't remember. Sometimes I think it was always there."

"Always?" I asked. "Someone had to give it to you."

She didn't answer, but instead focused on her food.

Looking at the marks, they didn't resemble any familiar pattern. Was it a tag of some sort, the way a rancher marks his livestock? Was it so the Union could spot her easier, should she ever get away from them? Maybe that was why the nun had placed her in a box, so that no one would see the mark and report them, but weren't there easier ways to track a person than a tattoo? And if that was the case, why didn't Abigail simply cover the mark with a cloth? Why not go to a back-alley surgeon and get it removed?

No, there had to be something else to it. Something I couldn't see.

Lex finished her soup, then stared at the empty bowl.

"You want some more?" I asked, seeing the hunger still in her eyes.

She looked at me, timidly. "Can I?"

"Sure thing, kid," I said, standing and going to the food dispenser. "Just do me a favor, would you?"

"Okay," she said.

"Next time you want something, just ask. Don't just wait for me to give it to you."

"Wouldn't that be rude?"

I laughed. "Kid, I know you've got a nun for a guardian, but take it from me. The galaxy ain't made for that kind of talk."

"It's not?"

I poured a fresh cup of soup and placed it in front of her. "In this life, you take what you need to survive. If you spend your days worrying about other people's feelings, you'll never make it anywhere. You get me?"

"Yeah," she said, staring at the steaming bowl sitting before her. "Thanks, Mr. Hughes."

* * *

"What a sight," said Hitchens, looking out the window of *The*

*Renegade Star.* "I never get tired of seeing this."

He was referring to the slip tunnel, of course, and I had to say I couldn't blame him. The walls of the passage were always so bright and colorful, with random bursts of what looked like lightning.

I watched the group of passengers huddle together to see the show as we passed through the tunnel. Abigail was the only one ignoring it, most likely because she'd just spent several months flying from one system to another. She'd probably had her fill of it by now.

"What happens if we go over there?" asked Lex, pointing to the tunnel wall.

"Bad things," said Fred, who was so young I could have been—well, not his father, but a much older brother, at least.

"Like what?" asked the girl.

Fred thought for a moment. "Think of slipspace like a river, Lex. Right now, we're following the flow, so it's pretty easy to keep going forward. If we move around too much, though, we could drop into another stream. If it's going in the opposite direction, the two currents could tear the ship apart."

"Oh," said Lex, and I was sure she didn't understand.

"There's more to it than that, of course," said Fred. "We don't always use these tunnels when we travel. They're simply the fastest method for long distance, although we can discuss that later."

He was wasting his time, trying to explain faster-than-light travel to a kid, but who was I to interrupt? Maybe some of it would sink into that head of hers.

"Listen up, tourists," I said, grabbing their attention. "We're about to arrive at the next S.G. Point. Might want to have a seat."

"Certainly, Captain Hughes," said Hitchens, a jolly grin on his face.

"Jace is fine, Doc," I said.

The group joined Abigail, strapping themselves into their seats around the lounge. Fred had to help Lex with her buckle, but after a few seconds, everyone was secure.

I returned to the cockpit to do the same. "Siggy, are we ready?"

"Dropping in five," said the A.I.

We came out of the tunnel, decelerating and raising the cloak. It took about four minutes to ready the next slip, so I pulled out another hard candy—orange this time—and unwrapped it.

I waited for Siggy to give me the go-ahead on the next jump as I eased back in my chair, watching the digital displays from the various cameras along the ship. One of them showed the previous tunnel entrance, still open, and with no sign of closing.

The blue and green colors flared inside, refusing to stop. I waited, expecting a change, except nothing happened. It wasn't closing.

"Siggy," I said, after more than a minute of this.

"Sir?" he asked.

I leaned on the dash, watching the display. "Why hasn't the tunnel collapsed yet? Are we too close to it?"

"I don't believe so, sir. We've moved far enough away that our position should have no effect on it."

"So, what's wrong? Why hasn't it stopped?"

"Barring some anomaly, I would hypothesize that another ship is about to arrive," he said.

"Another ship?" I asked.

"Based on the available data, that scenario seems the most likely, sir."

"Are we close to any space stations? Any colonies?" I asked.

"No, sir," said the A.I. "Not unless one was erected in the last three weeks, since my last update."

I debated moving *The Star* to a safer nearby location—maybe behind an asteroid or a moon—but there was no reason to panic. Not yet. This could have been anything. "Start the next slip, Siggy. Get us out of here."

"Right away," he said.

The cloak dropped and Siggy activated the slip drive, opening the next tunnel. I took us forward and into the rift, passing into the tunnel.

I was never one to panic, so I didn't jump to any immediate conclusions about who was behind us. In all likelihood, it was probably nobody. Maybe just a freighter or a ship on its way to some planet. Whatever the case, it had nothing to do with me, so there was no reason to worry.

At least, that's the story I told myself.

# EIGHT

There was a knock at my door and my eyes snapped open. "Captain, are you in there?" I heard the voice ask.

I looked at the time. To my surprise, I'd been asleep for nearly six hours. I usually didn't rest that long with passengers onboard.

"What is it?" I asked, sitting up and twisting around so my feet were on the floor.

"It's Frederick, sir," he said.

"What do you want, Fred?" I asked, reaching beneath my bed to grab a swig of water from my jug.

"I was hoping to talk to you, if you have a moment."

I got up and opened the door. He was a little shorter than me. Probably still growing, given his age. "What?" I asked, taking a drink.

His eyes widened as he stood there. "Shouldn't you put on some clothes?"

I glanced down at myself, then chuckled. "Whoops!"

Fred turned away. "I'm so sorry!"

I grabbed my pants. "It's fine. What do you want?"

"I had to make sure you were up-to-date on what the mission

is, once we arrive."

I buckled my belt, then grabbed my shirt. "What's it matter?"

"What's it...matter?" he asked, echoing my words.

"I'm just your ride, last I checked. A glorified taxi service."

"Is that what they told you?" he asked, peeking through his hand to see if I was dressed.

I raised my brow. "More or less."

"Oh," he said, finally looking at me. "The mission report I have states you're to join us on the surface. Your protective services are meant to extend beyond the confines of the ship."

"You mean those priests expect me to be your muscle, too?"

"Along with Sister Abigail," he said. "No one at the church has any experience with combat. She was the only one. I wouldn't worry, though. The only concern is the wildlife. No humans live there." He paused. "Well, not anymore."

I thought about the deal I'd struck with Loralin. She hadn't mentioned anything about me protecting these people. "No, this wasn't the deal," I said. "You call your boss and tell her I'll need more money."

"More money?" he asked.

"What is it? Worried they'll say no?" I asked.

"That's not it," he assured me. "It's just that we're too far out of range. The church isn't equipped with a high-grade com system. Instant communication won't be possible unless you're in a neighboring system."

I gave him a look.

He raised his hands. "But don't worry! I'm sure they'll agree once we return. I can speak on your behalf."

"Tell them I want another ten thousand. You got that?"

"Okay," he nodded.

I grinned. This deal was getting better every minute. "All right, kid. What was it you wanted to talk to me about?"

"Oh, right," he said, perking up. "I just wanted to brief you on a few details. Namely, the wildlife. It's not exactly pleasant, but as long as we stick to the path Doctor Hitchens has drawn here, we should be fine."

He handed me a pad with a map already displayed. It covered a good chunk of land, and the distance between the landing zone and our destination wasn't far. Maybe a two-hour walk. "Okay," I said, returning the device.

"The place we're going is in the mountain. It's something of a cave, I guess you'd say, except unnatural."

"Like ruins?" I asked.

"Exactly that," he said. "They've decayed so much that they're a part of the ground now. Sunken into the earth. We're not expecting any trouble, but it's better to have someone who knows how to handle themselves, just in case. I assume we can rely on you, Captain."

"Shouldn't be a problem," I said, nodding at the blaster sitting in its holster on my dresser. "I'm a good shot."

* * *

Not long after we found the planet, I ordered Sigmond to drop us on the landing zone—the exact spot Fred had specified.

The clearing—a field between two forests—was level enough for an easy landing. We disembarked and I told Sigmond to engage the cloak until we returned. No use taking any unnecessary risks with my ship.

Standing outside the cargo bay doors, Hitchens tapped my shoulder. He wore a large, goofy hat to shade himself, though I suspected he had no idea how ridiculous he looked. "That's our destination, Captain," said the doctor, pointing to a snow-tipped mountain to the east.

"I hope we're not climbing it," I commented.

"Certainly not," said Hitchens. He chuckled. "I'd never be able to do such a thing. No, we're heading to the base. An easy walk for someone like you, Captain. Less so for me."

We followed his directions, making our way through the woods. I had my blaster ready. I also had my earpiece with me, just in case Sigmond picked up any hostile movements, whether on land or in space.

As we walked, I noticed several pillars in the earth, clearly manmade. The majority were faded and broken, although a few stood tall. From what little I could tell, they had some kind of text carved into them, though centuries of rain had made them nearly impossible to make out.

I wondered, briefly, what these structures were for. Had there been a city here once, only to be wiped away? Or were the pillars simply extensions of something far larger, buried under the grass and dirt we were walking on? I tried to imagine a city beneath my feet, all its treasures lost forever.

None of it mattered anymore. Whoever built these things had long since vanished, forgotten like so many before them. Such was the cost of living.

A large wailing cry echoed in the distance, somewhere beyond the forest trees. "Did you hear that?" asked Fred, looking around.

"Just animals," I said, still walking. "Keep going."

"What if they attack?" he asked, scurrying after me.

"We can always shoot them."

"I'd rather avoid killing anything while we're here," said Doctor Hitchens. "Though, I suppose our own survival must come first."

"This guy gets it," I said, pointing my thumb at the plump doctor.

He chuckled. "I'm a conservationist when I can help it, but a pragmatist at heart."

I tapped my blaster. "You and me both, Doc."

\* \* \*

It took a few hours to reach the mountain. As we neared the cliff, the ground turned hard with stone, replacing the soft earth.

Lex tripped and fell, scaring half our group. Abigail ran to her, a look of panic and fear all over the nun's face. The girl hit the rocks, tumbling a bit, and ended up scraping her knee. I expected her to cry like every other kid, except to my surprise, there was nothing. The girl simply got back on her feet and continued, almost like nothing had happened.

I suspected she was used to pain, numb from all the time she'd spent in captivity, but I wouldn't ask her about it. A person's pain was their own business. It was best to let them carry it in silence.

A short walk later we were standing in front of a cavern, pillars and carvings all around us. Hitchens proceeded first, climbing down into the cave, his assistant Octavia holding his hand to steady him. I was right beside them, my blaster out and ready.

We reached the bottom, although it was difficult to see. "Hold a second," said the doctor, and he took out a small device. With the press of a button, the little machine emitted a light so bright, it brought most of the darkened cave to life. Suddenly, I could see everything around us—dozens of buried machines, inoperable and long-decayed. Above us, a covering of stone and stalactites. Whatever this place used to be, the world had taken it back, merging stone and metal.

"Come down, everyone," said Hitchens.

Lex, Abigail, and Fred descended the rock, being careful to watch their footing.

"How long before we get there?" asked Lex.

"It's not far now," said Hitchens. "Just beyond here."

We followed the doctor's lead as he passed by the various machines, ignoring them. Whatever he was after, it was clearly more important than any of this.

As we crept further into the cavern, I began to see the remains of several animal nests. They were comprised of twigs, wires, and metal. Several pieces of broken eggshell lay scattered across the nests, covered in dust.

We made our way through two long corridors, and to my surprise, I began to see lights along the walls and inside machines. Somehow, the technology here was still active and operational, though I couldn't say what it did, if anything.

"This way," said Hitchens, motioning for us to enter another opening. The door to this room was laying on the ground nearby, cracked and half-sunk. It was thick and made of metal, too big to move.

The doctor shined his device on the center of the room, revealing a table and what I gleaned to be a star map—a half-circular device with a grid on the top. A small light blinked on its side. Beside it, I saw a reclining chair, attached to the machine. "What is this place?" I muttered.

"We call it the Cartographer," said Hitchens.

He turned to the nearby console, which was covered in dust, yet still operational. He retrieved a small card from his satchel, then placed it on the machine's surface.

I watched as the blinking light went solid, going from blue to emerald green. The circular grid at the center of the table flickered before finally solidifying and lighting up. "Here we are," said the good doctor.

We stared at the machine as it came to life. A hologram of the galaxy manifested before our eyes, two hundred billion stars blinking into existence within mere seconds.

I craned my neck back to see the full span of the image. "You came all this way for a map of the galaxy?"

"Hardly," said Abigail.

Hitchens motioned for Lex to come closer. "My dear, if you would please take a seat right here."

Lex nodded and went to the ancient, reclined chair. She climbed into it so that her feet dangled off the edge, then leaned back and stared up into the rock ceiling.

"Fantastic," said Hitchens.

Abigail went to the girl's side and held her hand. "Everything will be fine. You're doing a wonderful job."

Lex smiled. "Okay."

Hitchens entered a command into the console, and I heard a clicking sound, as though something had just turned on. "Command acknowledged," said a female voice I didn't recognize.

"The hell was that?" I asked, yanking out my blaster.

"Easy," said Abigail. "It's just the computer."

"Oh," I said, holstering my weapon.

"She's not as sophisticated as your typical A.I.'s," said Hitchens. He typed something into the console. "Let's see if we can just—"

"Command acknowledged," said the voice.

"Ah, there we are," said the doctor, smiling. He twisted in his seat to look at Lex. "Stay perfectly still, dear."

"Okay," said Lex.

A light emitted from beneath the chair, and I watched as it moved from her head to her feet, then back again, finally stopped at the point just below her neck.

"Fiducial recognized," said the voice. "Initiating data retrieval."

Lex looked at Abigail, who continued to hold her hand. "Almost done," said the nun.

The hologram display blinked, disappearing briefly, as though it were resetting, and then returned. Suddenly, a string of stars changed from white to red, forming a single line, beginning at our present location and stretching halfway across the galaxy.

The light faded from beneath Lex, and I saw her face relax. "Process complete," said the voice.

Everyone stared up at the star chart before us. "We have it!" exclaimed Fred. He clapped his hands. "After all this time, there it is!"

"It seems the wait was well worth it," remarked Hitchens.

I looked at each of them. "Can someone tell me what just happened? What is this thing?"

"Isn't it obvious?" asked Octavia, who had been rather silent before now. "It's a map."

"You came all this way for a map?"

"Captain Hughes, I beg your pardon," said Doctor Hitchens, a genuinely happy look on his face. "This isn't just any map, my friend. Far from it."

"Okay, so what's the deal? What could possibly be so important that you needed a map in an old cave to show you where to go?" I paused for a second. "And why the hell did that kid just sit in that chair?"

"So now you want to know?" asked Abigail. "I thought you didn't care about our mission."

Fred walked over to me. "Mr. Hughes, do you know what the Church of the Homeworld is?"

*A cult,* I thought, but didn't say it. "A religious group. I don't know."

Fred shook his head. "We're not a religion. We're—"

"Hey!" snapped Abigail, staring at the young man.

"It's okay. We owe it to him for taking us this far," said Fred. He looked back at me. "The Church of the Homeworld is more than just a fringe sect, Mr. Hughes. We're a scientific organization devoted to a singular goal."

"Which is?" I asked.

"The eventual discovery of the origin point of all Mankind," said Fred. "The mythical lost world known as Earth."

* * *

I couldn't believe what I was hearing as we stood in the decaying cavern of a lost civilization. "Earth," I muttered, trying not to take any of this seriously. "You're looking for Earth."

"That's right," said Doctor Hitchens.

"The fairytale planet that no one has ever seen. The one where people used to fight dragons and use magic. That Earth."

"We don't believe in those parts," remarked Fred. "But much like other myths, we believe the seed of this one to have some truth to it."

"So you think Earth is real and this—" I motioned at the hologram above my head. "—thing, this map, is going to show you how to get there?"

"Correct," said Hitchens. "In fact, today confirms it."

"How are you so confident?" I asked.

He paused and looked at Lex, then again at me. "We have our reasons. Perhaps if you—"

A scream filled the cave, forcing me to shield my ears. "What the fuck!" I shouted.

The cry continued, coming from somewhere near the

entrance. "I think it's an animal," said Fred, pulling out his scanner. "I can't read anything from here."

"What do we do?" asked Hitchens.

I drew my pistol, taking aim at the open doorway. "Stay behind me," I told them.

Abigail came to my side, taking out her own weapon—an eight-shooter Artesian handgun, by the look of it. I wanted to snap at her for bringing a pistol onboard my ship, but decided against it. I'd yell at her later when we weren't under attack by a pack of wild animals. "I hope your aim is good," I said.

"Better than yours," she returned.

I heard another howl, this time closer. A shadow moved from beyond the opening, and I squeezed the trigger tight.

* * *

The monsters rushed into the room, their snarling jaws full of foam and raging.

I turned one into a corpse with a single shot to the skull. Three more appeared instantly, charging at our group.

Abigail hit the first in the leg and chest, staggering it a moment before the final bullet plunged into the animal's snout, sending chunks of its brains into the nearby wall.

I set my sights on the other two, firing without hesitation. Seven shots left the barrel of my gun, each with a distinct purpose, each one piercing flesh.

The beasts collapsed, almost simultaneously, sliding into one another. I continued firing with precision, hitting every living member of the pack as it came.

A pile of bodies formed a meter in front of the entrance, blocking our view. I saw one of the beasts leap over its fallen brothers, a hunger in its eyes. It came down on Abigail, its jaw ready to snap her in two, but she raised her gun and fired into it.

The beast fell on her, knocking her back, and for the first time I saw how truly massive the animals were. This one covered most of her body. I could barely see Abigail.

She rolled the animal off of her, revealing spots of blood from where the bullets had pierced its gut. I helped her to her feet, and she wiped her forehead. Her hands were shaking, but her face was calm. *Not bad for a nun,* I thought.

I gave her a slight nod, then returned my gaze to the entryway, raising my pistol, and waiting.

There was nothing after that. Only the silent dead.

# NINE

We waited for Hitchens to download the map to his device before we left. Hardly anyone spoke a word until we were out of the cave.

With the exception of myself and Abigail, I doubted any of the others had any real combat experience. Seeing their expressions, full of confusion and fear, reminded me that not everyone had the skill to survive out here. Not on their own.

Abigail, who still had stains of animal blood on her clothes, walked alongside Lex. The girl's composure continued to impress me. She never cried, never showed an ounce of panic. I couldn't help but wonder why.

We reached the woods soon enough, finally free of the confines of the cave, and I told the group to rest. It would take us two full hours to make it back to *The Star*, and it was clear some of them needed the break.

"I appreciate it," wheezed Hitchens, trying to catch his breath. He sat beneath a large tree, fanning himself with his hat.

Octavia took out a canteen of water and passed it to him. "Here you are, sir," she said.

He gulped it down, spilling some on his shirt. "Thank you, my dear."

I looked at Fred, waving him over.

"Yes, sir?" said the young scholar.

"Don't think I forgot what you told me back there," I said, motioning in the direction of the cave. "That story about Earth? The nonsense with the map? I still want to know what the deal with this kid is, too."

"O-Of course," stuttered Fred.

"There's more to all this," I said, raising my brow. "A *lot* more."

"Well," he began, a look of hesitation on his face. "I can't exactly tell you everything. I think that's up to the council."

"Oh?" I asked.

He held his hands up. "But they will, I'm sure. Don't worry. You saved all our lives. You're a hero, Mr. Hughes."

"I'm a hired gun," I corrected.

He nodded. "R-Right, of course. My point is just that you were vital to our success today. The council will see that, and they'll likely ask you for further assistance."

I tilted my head. "Further assistance?"

"That's right. We'll need help if we're to pursue those coordinates. You saw where the trail went, didn't you? It's on the other side of ravager territory. We'll need your cloak to make it."

"Hold on a sec, kid. I never agreed to anything besides this one job. I've got things I need to do."

"Even if the money is there?" he asked.

"We'll see how I feel about the offer when they make it," I answered.

"Typical Renegade," said Abigail.

Fred and I turned to see her standing a few meters away.

"You're only out for yourself. Didn't you hear what the doctor said?" asked the nun.

"You mean about Earth?" I asked, smirking. "The make-believe planet that doesn't exist?"

"It *does* exist. You saw the map. Open your eyes."

"All I saw was a standard galactic star chart with a few blinking lights. Nothing special. Definitely nothing that told me one of them was Earth."

"Give him time," said Fred. "He hasn't seen what you've seen, Sister."

"That's right, *Sister*," I said, winking. "Quit picking on me."

"You're hopeless," she said, dismissively, and then walked back over to where Lex was sitting.

"That nun sure is something else," I said.

"She is," Fred agreed. "Wait until you really make her mad. I heard she killed six men when she rescued Lex."

"Now *that* I can believe."

* * *

"Strap in and hold on tight," I said over the com, sitting in the cockpit of *The Renegade Star*. "Siggy, take us up and out."

"Right away, sir," said the A.I.

The engines primed and I felt my seat tremble. The ship began to lift off, and I watched the green field fade into a distant blur. We withdrew into the sky, finally, and I leaned back in my seat, thrilled to be done with this place.

The orange horizon turned purple and then black as we entered the thermosphere. A few moments later, we broke orbit.

"Take us to Arcadia, Siggy," I said.

"Inputting coordinates," he said, and I watched as the star chart transformed to reflect our route.

A short while later, the opening of a slip tunnel formed before me. As we entered the swirling mass of blue and green slipspace, I suddenly felt exhausted.

I looked down at my hands. They were dirty, covered in grime and, to my surprise, a bit of blood. *I need a shower,* I thought, then pushed myself out of the chair. "Siggy, call me if there's an emergency."

"Yes, sir," he responded.

In the lounge, several of my guests had convened, with only Abigail and Lex absent from the group.

"Ah, Captain," said Hitchens, waving at me.

"Talk to Sigmond if you need anything," I said, dismissively. "I need to sleep."

"I was hoping to talk with you about—"

"Sleep," I said, holding my hand up.

He sat there with his mouth partially open, then shut it, nodding.

I went straight into my tiny room and stripped, ready to wash this stench off and pass out.

* * *

I woke up drooling, coming out of a deep sleep. It felt like I'd been dead, my body was so stiff and tense.

"Siggy, how long was I out?" My throat was dry, so I took a drink from my water jug.

"Ten and a half hours, sir," said the A.I.

"Holy shit," I muttered. "Guess I needed that."

"It seems so," said Sigmond.

I slipped on my pants and left the bed as it was, the blankets tossed and partially on the floor. I didn't bother putting on a shirt.

The lounge was empty, save for Fred, who sat alone, sipping coffee. "Good morning," he said with a genuine smile.

"Piss off," I answered. "Pour me a cup of that, would you?"

"Of course," he said.

I sat in my favorite chair and rubbed my eyes. "Everyone else asleep?"

"It's early," he said, placing a cup on the table.

I didn't drink any yet. Instead, I took a long sniff and inhaled the aroma, waiting for it to cool. The coffee on my ship wasn't the best, but it smelled like a drug.

Fred sat across from me, sipping on his own and continuing to read his pad.

"Any news in the Union?" I asked. "You know it's all propaganda."

"Oh, I agree. These are just notes. I've been researching slipspace technology and theoretical applications for it. There's some promising papers in circulation."

I groaned, finally taking a drink. "Let me get my head on straight before you get into all that."

"Sorry," he said.

"It's fine." I took another drink and let out a relaxed sigh. "God, this is good."

"You should try the stuff we have on Arcadia. I've never had coffee so good."

"Oh, yeah?" I asked, suddenly interested.

"They bring it in once a month, along with a bunch of other supplies. All high-grade products from Din."

I knew the name immediately. Din was home to a merchant organization known as the Dinesian Trading Company. They specialized in consumables, specifically across Union space, and like every other major corporate entity, they had an underbelly. The DTC had its hands in smuggling exotic goods—a business tactic the Union wasn't keen on. Still, that didn't stop them, and they outsourced the job to guys like me who were happy to accept the credits. "That's gotta cost you a pretty credit or two."

He nodded. "It does, indeed."

"Let me ask you this, Fred," I said, taking another sip. "How's a weird little cult like yours get so much money? Did you trick a few old ladies into emptying their purses?"

Fred laughed. "Have you heard of a man named Darius Clare?"

I said that I didn't.

"He was a Union archaeologist about a century ago," said Fred. "He worked for a special department within the government. Their mission was to investigate reports of unknown relics and fantastic oddities, wherever they were found."

"And?" I asked, unimpressed.

"Well, he and his team operated all over known space, traveling to nearly sixty planets in pursuit of knowledge. They uncovered many fascinating antiques that couldn't be explained. Most were catalogued by the Union, stuffed in storage, and never seen again. A few—" He paused, giving me a sly grin. "—went missing."

"Is this going somewhere?" I asked, taking another drink, only to realize the cup was empty. I frowned. "I'm not a big history buff."

"I assure you, it all matters."

I got up and poured another cup. "Fine."

Fred continued. "On a certain dig, Darius and a woman named Reslin Gaile, his partner and future wife, uncovered a two thousand-year-old storage device. They thought nothing of it at first, since such machines were common in digs like this and typically yielded nothing of true importance. Usually, you might find a log entry or someone's personal diary. Historically interesting for scholars, although not exactly pertinent to Darius's mission." Fred leaned in. "However, when he and his partner returned to their lab, they began the process of retrieving the stored data within the device. It took several weeks to fully reconstruct the data within. When they finally did, they discovered a message."

"What did it say?" I asked.

"Earth is restored. Initiate Project Reclamation."

"What does that mean?" I asked, setting my cup down.

"That's what Darius wanted to know. He was thrilled about this discovery, so he returned to his superiors to try and get their backing on expanding the project, this time with more focus. He wanted to search for more clues about Earth."

"Let me guess," I said. "They told him to piss off."

"No, not at first. The Union leadership was actually intrigued by the data Darius collected. They continued to fund his efforts and even elected him as the head of the department. He kept working for them for another twelve years, searching for relics related to Earth, expanding his team, and acquiring more leads."

"What happened?"

"He failed to deliver anything substantial. After a while, his superiors lost faith in him. They let him go."

I chuckled. "Figures."

Fred gave me a wry smile. "Does it? Darius knew what the Union was after. He'd found data on Earth's lost technology, and he knew what the government would do once they had it. He took his research and left the organization, but he didn't give up on any of it. He and several members of his team continued to search for the truth. They made it their mission to discover the homeworld." He looked down at the pad in his hand and smiled. "Years after he left his job, Darius discovered an archive full of information deep inside some ancient catacombs beneath a mountain on a small colony world, far removed from Union space. Among the priceless data, there was a single image that stood out."

He turned the pad around to show me what he was looking at—a planet, blue and green with expansive continents. I didn't recognize it, despite my many travels. "What's that?" I asked, taking the pad from him, and looking closer.

"Isn't it obvious?" asked Freddie, and I knew that it was. "This is where we all came from, Mr. Hughes. This is *Earth*."

# TEN

I didn't believe half of what Fred told me. Hell, I wasn't sure I even understood it. An undiscovered planet with boundless treasure, hidden for two thousand years, and it just so happened to be the legendary origin point of the entire human race?

Please. I wasn't your everyday sucker, not like the rest of these fools. I could already see where they were leading me, trying to convince me of some grand lie, just so they wouldn't have to pay me what I was owed. Help the cause, they'd tell me, only I was no stranger to money schemes. Maybe they really did believe all of this. Maybe they were all good people.

But I wasn't about to give up my fee for the betterment of mankind, even if it *was* all true. I had a debt to pay off.

I sat in my bunk, sucking on a piece of candy, replaying the events on Epsilon as they had happened. I thought about Lex as she'd sat in that chair, and the ancient machine that sparked to life, revealing a line of dots from one end of the galaxy to the other.

*Bullshit*, I thought, lying back and scratching my nose.

"Excuse me, sir," said Sigmond, his voice coming on over the speaker in my room.

"What is it, Siggy?" I asked.

"We are nearing the end of the final tunnel," he explained.

"Thanks for the heads-up," I said. "Tell the cult to grab their shit and get ready."

"You have a way with words, sir," said Sigmond.

Siggy wouldn't say it exactly like that. I knew he'd ease up on the vulgarity. He always did. Sometimes you just have to express yourself, even when no one besides you can hear the words you're saying.

I slid out of the bed and got to my feet. "Can't wait to get this job behind me, Siggy. The sooner we get paid, the sooner I can get my debt squared with Fratley."

"Of course, sir. I know how you hate getting involved with other people."

"Are you getting a tone with me?" I asked. Despite only being an A.I., Siggy understood me. Maybe it was all the time we'd spent together or the fact he was built to adjust to his owner's personality, but he knew how to mess with me the way a friend would. He understood my limits.

"I would never dream of such a thing," he said.

I touched the button next to my door, then waited as it slid open. "Just remember, we don't have time to be hospitable. We have to get that money and hightail it straight to Fratley. The sooner, the better, lest I lose this boat and everything in it, including you."

"I'd rather not have that happen, sir."

"You and me both."

As I made my way through the ship, I could hear Sigmond telling each of the passengers what was about to happen. They scurried about, trying to gather their things, filling the ship with commotion.

I entered the cockpit and took my seat. It had taken us two days to return. To my surprise, it felt like we'd only just left.

The ship trembled, a sign we'd emerged from the tunnel. I glanced out the nearest window to see the darkness of space, stars in the distance.

Bending slightly, I tried to see if I could spot Arcadia.

As it slowly came into view, I imagined my account filling with credits. Fifty thousand. One hundred thousand. It would all depend on how much I could squeeze out of that council. These people were a gold mine.

Fred had asked me to stay with them for another job once this was done, but I still hadn't decided. If I took the work, I'd have to leave and return later. I couldn't let the debt stand for too long. Not if I valued my life. As soon as I could, probably later tonight, I'd go straight to Fratley and give him his money.

The edge of the planet floated across the glass, growing as we neared.

Something was different now, I noticed. The once quiet world of Arcadia now had several ships waiting in orbit.

I stared at them, curiously. Were they a part of the trade shipments Fred had mentioned? No...they didn't match the design. These were sharp, triangular vessels. Green flames in white circles had been painted along their hulls.

They were ravager ships.

My skin crawled as I stood there, balking through the glass. What were ravagers doing here? Why would they go after a worthless religious group? Were they—

Before I could finish the thought, I felt the entire floor drop, thrusting me against the wall. An explosion shocked the ship and an alarm rang throughout the corridors.

"Sigmond!" I shouted. "Cloak us and get us the fuck out of here!"

"Right away, sir," he answered.

Abigail came running out of her room from the other end of the lounge. "What was that?!"

"We're under attack. There's a fleet of ravagers out there," I said, pointing in the direction of the planet.

"Ravagers?" she asked. "What did you do?"

"Me?" I scoffed. "What makes you think *I* did something?"

"Sir, the cloak has been activated, but I'm receiving a hail," announced Sigmond. "Should I accept?"

"Throw it on speaker."

Lex joined Abigail in the hall. "What is it?" asked the girl.

"Nothing," said Abigail. "We're handling it."

"*I'm* handling it," I corrected.

"Sir, the channel is open. You are receiving, but we are not transmitting," said Sigmond.

"Let's hear it," I said.

A second later, a familiar voice came through the ship's speaker. "Jace Hughes," said the man I knew as Fratley. "It's about time you showed up. I've been waiting."

\* \* \*

Fratley was the last person I expected to hear on the com today. I still had some time on the clock before my debt was due. What was he doing here?

"Jace," said Fratley, his voice echoing through the entire ship. "Talk to me, you old thief. You think you can hide with the cloak I gave you? You ought to know better than that."

"Does that mean he can see us?" asked Abigail.

"I don't know," I muttered.

"Jace, you done me wrong. You done me *so* wrong," said Fratley. "Owing me money is one thing, but you killed two of my men back at Galdion. Did you think I wouldn't notice it was you? Then you come out here to the Deadlands, trying to hide from me. That's a coward's way, Jace, but what should I expect of a man who came asking for a cloak, of all things."

I felt my chest sink. "Shit," I said, pressing my knuckles into the wall, cracking them.

"Now, you know I'm a fair guy, Jace. I ain't one to hold a grudge, except you owe me a heaping pile of credits and I need 'em bad," said Fratley. "You shot down two of my ships, and I'll let it go if you're willing to pay up twice what you owe. You following me, Jace? You hear what I'm saying?"

"That piece of shit," I said.

"One hundred thousand. You got that much in creds?" asked Fratley.

"Sigmond, start transmitting," I ordered.

"Yes, sir. Just a moment," said Sigmond. "Go ahead, sir."

"Fratley, it's me," I said.

"Ah! There he is!" exclaimed Fratley.

I took a breath. "How you been?" I asked, trying to sound relaxed. "I was just on my way to talk to you. Thanks for saving me the time."

"Does that mean you have my creds?"

"I've got a bit, just not everything. That kind of money takes time."

"That's not what I need to hear, Jace. I was hoping to have a good day today, but you've gone and disappointed me already. You killed my men, blew up my ships, so now you owe me for my loss. Don't try to weasel your way out of it, either. I've seen the holos. I know that was you at Galdion."

"Fratley, let's be reasonable," I said. "Those two ships attacked me when I was leaving the planet on a job. A job, I might add, that I had to take in order to pay you back. Besides, they fired at me first. What was I supposed to do?"

"I'll tell you one thing, Jace. You *don't* shoot down my fighters. That's what you *don't* do," said Fratley.

"How about I pay you twenty-five thousand now, then get you the rest later?" I asked. "I'm working a job and about to take another. I can pay you with interest when they're both done."

"Oh, now that's what I like to hear. You know, Jace, I had one of my fighters following you for a while. I had to make sure you weren't running out of the Deadlands, trying to get away."

"You followed me?" I asked, remembering the slip tunnel from before and how it hadn't closed immediately.

"You know it's just business, Jace," he said. "Don't worry. I saw where you went. Some abandoned planet with a bunch of old ruins. I figured you must be pulling an escort job. I can respect that, except..." He paused, and I heard him lick his lips. "I gotta ask you, Jace. Were you working for anyone on *this* planet? Because that'd be pretty unfortunate."

"Why? What's it matter?"

"Oh, Jace, you poor bastard," said Fratley with a laugh. "I'm sorry to tell you, but I was getting impatient, sitting around here for you to come back. I sent my boys down there already, and man, they've been busy killing. Been busy killin' all *day*!"

My eyes widened as I slowly looked at Abigail. Her mouth was open and she appeared horrified, ready to say something. I pressed my finger to my lips and, to her credit, she kept her composure, at least for the time being.

I took a slow breath, trying to keep my head. I knew Fratley was a piece of shit, but murdering a random group of civilians was something else altogether. "Fratley, call your men off. I need those people alive. It's the only way you'll get your money."

"I'm afraid I can't do that, Jace. You see, we came out this way looking for you, and we've been waiting here a while. My men need a chance to cut loose, though, so things got a little messy. You know how it is."

Lex looked up at Abigail, about to say something, but the nun motioned for her to stay quiet. The two of them stared at me. "Fratley, if you let them die, how am I supposed to pay you?"

"I guess you can't," said Fratley, laughing a little. "Boy, ain't you in a predicament? I'd hate to be in your sorry ass shoes."

"Godsdammit," I muttered.

"Tell you what, Jace. I'll give you a few more days to collect what you owe. Just go murder some folks and steal what they got. That's easy work for a guy like you, ain't it?"

"Sure thing, Fratley. I can do that." I had no chance at salvaging this situation. The best thing I could do was agree to his terms and run like hell.

"Good man. Now, you mind telling me what you were doing for these priests? What kind of work did they have you on?"

"I glanced at Abigail and Lex. They stared back at me with

terrified expressions. "I was asked to make sure the way was clear for a trip they wanted to take. I was coming back to pick them up."

"Too bad for you," said Fratley. "Maybe next time you'll work faster."

"I will," I agreed, sounding complacent. "Anyway, I'd best get going if I'm to pay you what I owe. One hundred thousand credits, I think it was."

Fratley laughed. "Right you are, Jace! Oh, but before you do, I'll have to ask you to wait a few minutes. My boys need to search that piece of shit ship of yours."

"Search my ship? Come on, is that really necessary? I don't have anything here. All that'll do is slow us both down."

"Call it punishment for making me wait," said Fratley.

*Shit*, I thought. *If he finds Abigail and the others on here, he'll kill them just to get to me.*

"Expect a boarding party in ten minutes," said Fratley. "And Jace, you better not try to fuck with me again. You understand?"

"I wouldn't dream of it," I said, looking out the window at the fleet of ravager ships.

The speaker clicked off. "The channel has been cut by the other party," said Sigmond.

I looked at Abigail and Lex, standing there together. Behind them, Fred, Hitchens, and Octavia were waiting, all their eyes on me. They must have been standing there the entire time, but I hadn't even notice them.

"The—the church…" muttered Fred. "Are they…?"

"Don't think about that," I told him. "There's no time for grief right now." If Fratley discovered any of them on my ship, he'd kill everyone just for being in my proximity. He wouldn't care.

*Godsdammit.*

"This is because of us, isn't it?" asked Hitchens.

I grabbed the doctor's satchel from the couch and tossed it at him. The bag hit him in the chest, but Octavia managed to sweep it up. "Everyone, grab your shit, and I mean everything, and come with me."

"Are you turning us over to them?" asked Abigail, her voice far steadier than the rest.

"Don't be an idiot," I said. "They'd kill you, and probably me, too."

"So, what's the plan?" asked Octavia.

I walked over to the wall near the cockpit door, then tapped my knuckles against the metal. "See this?"

"The wall?" asked Fred.

I nodded. "Siggy, open it."

"Right away, sir."

Just then, the metal on the wall transformed, sliding back into itself, revealing a hidden storage area that extended beneath the entire lounge. "Store your shit and get ready for a tight squeeze."

"What is that?" asked Abigail.

"Most call this kind of thing a smuggler's bin," I said. "Today it's your salvation."

"I'm not certain I can fit," said Doctor Hitchens.

"I've got another spot to put you," I assured him. "I use it for the bulkier goods. Now, quick, get every single bag you've got and bring it here. We don't have much time."

Everyone raced to their rooms, returning momentarily, one at a time with their luggage. Even Lex had a small package in tow, although she didn't seem anxious, much to my surprise. "You good, kid?" I asked.

"I'm hungry," she answered. "Can I have some more tomato soup?"

I smirked. "Tell you what. You do what I say and you can have your fill in a few hours. Sound good?"

She smiled. "Okay!"

We stuffed as many bags into the wall that we could fit, while still leaving enough room for Abigail, Lex, and Freddie. The three of them crawled inside, maneuvering around the luggage and squeezing beneath the floor beneath us. They laid on their backs, staring up at us through the cracks in the flooring. "Everyone comfortable?" I asked, tapping where I was certain Abigail's face was watching.

"We're all set," she responded in a muffled voice.

I gave Siggy the order to close the wall. "Don't say a word until the ship is clear."

"We understand," said Abigail.

I turned to Hitchens and Octavia. "Now for you two."

The three of us went quickly to the cargo bay. "In here?" asked Hitchens.

I nodded. "Siggy, if you'd be so kind."

The hidden door slid open in the back, behind a series of crates. "I'll need some help moving these," I told the two archaeologists.

The three of us hoisted one of the boxes out of the way, which took longer than I expected. When we'd finished, I could see the strain in Hitchen's face. He was already sweating profusely, breathing like he'd run a marathon. The fat doctor leaned against the box, but I pointed at the hiding spot. "No time to stop. Get in there and don't say a word. You understand?"

Hitchens wiped his forehead with a handkerchief. "Yes, yes. Of course, Captain."

"Good. Now, hurry up," I said.

The two of them got inside and I watched as the door slid shut.

"Sir, Fratley's ship is signaling us to dock," announced Sigmond.

"Just in time," I answered. "Tell him we're ready for him."

I turned and raced out of the bay, my heart nearly beating out of my chest.

# Eleven

The ravager shipped docked with *The Star*, and a dozen armed men in red armor entered through the airlock.

Behind them, a man with a thin beard and thick eyebrows followed. He wore a small, round hat with gold trim. In his left hand, he held a thin cane with primitive carvings, something he'd picked up on a backwater planet. He carried it, not because he needed the assistance, but because he simply enjoyed the design. "Jace!" exclaimed the man, giving him a wide and unsettling smile. "If it isn't my favorite swindler."

"Hello, Fratley," I said, watching as he strode through the outer hall.

Fratley walked right up to me and gave me several pats on the shoulder. "There he is, my old friend. You ought to have gotten me and my boys some drinks while you waited."

I didn't bother smiling. "There's coffee."

He ignored me and continued further in, ogling the ship like it was his first time seeing it. "My, what a fine shithole you've made of this bucket."

"What can I say? I like to decorate," I said, walking slowly behind him.

He waltzed into the lounge and collapsed into one of the chairs. "Ah, now that's the stuff." He rubbed his hand along the fabric.

"Glad you like it," I said.

"You spoil yourself, Jace. I hope you're not spending the money you owe me on fancy chairs."

I said nothing. Fratley knew full well that I hadn't changed much about this ship before I got it. The only exceptions were a few things in my personal room, the coffee maker, Sigmond's neural core, and of course, the cloaking device.

He grinned at the armed ravager nearest to him. "What do you think? Should we take these seats back to the ship?" asked Fratley, laughing. "Nah, I'm just playing. We've got ourselves a nice setup back on the ship, don't we, boys?"

"Did you want to see the rest of the ship?" I asked.

"Oh, Jace, you always know just what to say. Sure! Let's see this piece of shit in full detail. Why not?" He got to his feet, slamming his cane on the floor. The action gave me pause, and I half-expected Lex or Abigail to scream.

But there was nothing, thankfully. It seemed those two had enough composure to stay quiet. Good for me, since I wasn't ready to die today.

I took Fratley and his men through the ship, showing them all the spots I wanted them to see. When we reached my room, there wasn't much to see, although that didn't stop his goons from tossing the dresser and mattress. In under a minute, I had sheets and clothes soaking in a pile of spilled water on the floor. I stared down at the jug I kept under my bed, quickly burying the anger.

Fratley only laughed. "They're rough, but they get the job done. Don't you agree, Jace?"

"Whatever works for you," I said.

"Show me what you got in your cargo hold," he ordered.

I did as he asked, and we stepped into the bay. As we entered, I felt a hand on my shoulder, holding me back. I looked to see one of the ravager men glaring at me to stay put.

Fratley continued into the room, his cane spinning in his hand. He looked around, clicking his tongue as he scanned the bay. "Tsk, tsk, Jace," he said, shaking his head. "Doesn't seem like you've had much work come your way. Big shame about those priests. I almost feel bad for killing them."

I tried not to look at the section of the wall where I knew Hitchens and Octavia were hiding. "I'll find more. Don't worry about it."

He looked at me from over his shoulder. "I'm sure you will."

Fratley glanced around, his eyes jumping from one item to the next. I had several crates in here, mostly filled with tools and random shit I'd found. In other words, junk. I expected him to start rummaging through it all, maybe have his guys toss a few boxes. Instead, he eyed something beneath the railing. Something close to where Hitchens and Octavia were hiding.

That was when my heart sank. I'd left a crate out, the one we'd pulled away so the two of them could squeeze inside the wall. Did Fratley see it? Did he realize how out of place it was?

I tried to move so I could see what he was looking at, but the ravager thug kept his hand firmly on my shoulder. I could always turn around and kick his ass, but so many of his goons behind him, I was pretty sure I'd wind up a corpse.

For now, all I could do was watch and hope the bastard didn't put the pieces together.

Fratley tapped his cane as he walked over to where the crate was sitting. He leaned in and looked behind it, saying nothing, and then banged the tip of his cane against the crate. "Now, why's this one out of place, I wonder?" he asked, leaning forward to examine it.

"It wasn't strapped in properly," I lied. "You know how those slip tunnels are sometimes. I hit some turbulence on my way out."

He waved his stick at the men next to me. "Let's pop it open, boys."

Three of them ran to his side like the eager dogs they were and attempted to open the lid. When it proved too difficult, they just knocked the crate on its side, spilling its guts onto the floor.

We all watched as several dozen pieces of clothing fell out of the box, each one air-sealed in plastic. "What's all this?" asked Fratley. "You smuggling shirts now?"

The group of ravagers laughed.

"Those are from a job I pulled a while back. The client gave me some as payment," I said.

"They paid you in clothes?" he asked, still laughing. "Damn, Jace. You just can't catch a break!"

I wasn't lying. The contents of the crate really had come from a client—a man named Arte who asked me to steal some high-end luxury apparel from a corporation called P&G Inc. Most of the clothes I delivered would sell well on the open market, except for these. This particular set of outfits were part of the discount line, which meant they were worthless. Arte let me keep them as a bonus, but I had no use for them. They weren't even worth the time it would take to sell them.

Fratley left the clothes on the floor, ignoring the rest of the cargo bay. "I think we're done here," he said as he neared me.

"Thanks for stopping by," I said.

He paused, a knowing smile on his face. "Since you've been a good boy today, I'm gonna be straight with you, Jace."

"Straight with me?"

He nodded. "We came out here for you, but that's not why I dropped so much fire on that church."

I raised my brow, saying nothing.

"Y'see, there's a warrant circling the gal-net. Seems the Union's after a nun, and the picture they got shows her dressed in the same outfit as the kind these people wear." He motioned for one of his men to hand him a pad, then showed it to me. Sure enough, it was Abigail, dressed in religious uniform. It looked like it was taken from security footage. "This is her, a few days after she broke into a Union lab and kidnapped a little girl. Can you believe that, Jace? Who does a thing like that?" He gave me a crooked smile.

"That's weird," I said, plainly.

"Warrant says the nun killed a man on her way out. A senator, from what I heard."

"That so?" I asked, trying to sound like I didn't care.

"This lady is supposed to be some kind of dangerous assassin, only I guess she ain't too good with keeping herself hidden. Union cameras picked her up a few more times after this." He tapped the pad and showed me another picture. "Sounds like bullshit, right? An assassin nun. Who would've thought?"

"That's pretty wild. I hope you catch her."

"I'll tell you what's *wild*, Jace. I come out here to talk to you and I see you working for the same church as this bitch. That's a *wild* coincidence, yeah? It really has me scratching my head."

His eyes went cold and serious as he glared at me.

I stared right back at him. If he thought he could intimidate me, this prick had another thing coming.

He chuckled. "Ah, I'm just teasing," he said, then slapped my shoulder. "I'm sure we'll turn something up on the surface, one way or another. If the girl ain't there, we'll find her."

"I'm sure you will."

He pointed his cane at me, nearly touching my forehead with the tip. "I'm giving you one more week to get me that money, by the way. Don't make me hunt you down again. I won't be so forgiving next time, you hear me?"

"I'll get you the money," I said, pushing the cane with my finger.

"I hope so, Jace. As much as I like you, I can't let a debt go unpaid. That's bad for business."

I watched Fratley and his crew leave through the airlock, making sure they could see me, and trying to look relaxed. I'd wait until their ship was fully detached before I let my stowaways out of their hiding spots. After that, I had no idea what I was going to do.

Fratley had given me a week to get his money. Who could say whether he'd left any survivors on the planet. I'd probably have to drop these people off on some rock, away from here, and find myself some credits, quickly.

Just when it seemed like everything was going to work out, the entire day just goes straight to shit.

Funny how that always happens.

\* \* \*

"Open it," I told Sigmond, and watched as the wall slid up to reveal the hidden compartment.

A drenched Abigail appeared inside, covered in sweat, and breathing heavily

"We need to talk," I said, stepping aside so she could come out.

"Are they gone?" she asked, climbing through the gap.

"For now, yeah, and you and I need to have a long conversation about just what is going on with—"

Lex popped her head from under the floor. "That was gross and smelly. I don't ever want to do that again."

I helped lift her out of the hole. When she was free, I tapped the wall and it closed. "As I was saying, we gotta talk."

Abigail went straight to the drink dispenser and tapped the button for water. She drank it so fast, I thought she might choke.

"Are you even listening to me?" I asked.

"Did you know it was that hot down there?" She filled the cup with water again and continued to drink.

"Sure I did, but it was the only option we had. Now, are you gonna answer my question or do I have to ask again?"

"I don't know what you're asking me," said the nun.

"Did you kill a man to save this kid?"

She stopped drinking. "What?"

"Fratley showed me a picture of you in the labs. He said you killed a senator. What the hell were you thinking?"

"I had no choice. I—" She paused, looking at Lex, hesitating to finish the thought. "Let's talk about this later, privately. I'll tell you everything."

"I'm not doing anything privately with you, lady. I'll talk to you and Fred together...and I want the truth this time." I turned toward the cockpit. "Siggy, go ahead and let the others out. Tell them to get in the lounge and plant their asses for a while, until I get us out of here."

"You're leaving the system?" asked Abigail, setting her empty cup on the table.

"Of course, I am. We're not staying here."

"You need to search for survivors at the church. There's safe spots all around the facility. You have to—"

"We can't worry about that right now. If Fratley sees me sitting here for much longer, it'll be all our asses."

She started to say something, only to shut her mouth. She hated the idea of running away, I was certain, but she also knew the reality of our situation.

"Just so you know," I continued. "I still aim to get paid for all this."

I left her there, taking my seat in the cockpit. I primed the engines and opened a new tear in slipspace.

# TWELVE

*The Renegade Star* sat floating in a loose orbit around the moon of Damos III, a system not far from Arcadia. The five members of the Church of the Homeworld, along with the little albino girl, sat together in the lounge, waiting for me to talk.

I didn't know what to say, except, "What the fuck is going on?"

Octavia got to her feet and looked at Lex. "Say, how about we go play for a bit?"

An eager smile formed on the young girl's face. "Okay!"

"I'll come and get you when we're done here," said Abigail.

"Take your time," answered Octavia as she and Lex began to leave.

As soon as they were gone, Abigail turned to face me again. "I'm happy to tell you everything, Mr. Hughes, but first I need some assurances."

"That's not how this works, nun. First, you tell me exactly what you're doing with this kid. After that, I'll decide if I want to assure you of anything."

"I can't just—"

"If you don't like it, there's the airlock." I pointed to the back half of the ship.

"I'm sure the Captain will understand," said Fred.

"Quite so," agreed Doctor Hitchens. "He's done a fine job of protecting us, wouldn't you agree?"

"He only did that because he was getting paid," said Abigail.

She was right. Before now, I'd been promised a payment. A rather large one at that. As it stood now, I had no reason to help these people, except the vague possibility of getting compensated for what I was owed. "I won't leave you stranded. How's that to start?"

Fred nodded. "See? There's no harm in telling him."

"Fine," resigned Abigail. "But you should know I'll kill you if you try to turn us in."

The woman was so frank, I nearly laughed. Not because it was funny, mind you. Only because I'd never met anyone with balls like hers. "You got it."

She took a breath. "Lex isn't your average little girl," she began. "She's part of something much larger."

"What do you mean?" I asked.

"Several years ago, back before the church first learned of her, Lex was a small child living on a fringe planet known as Deo. It's a farming world and thus remains of little interest to the Union. Lex was living there when a group of scientists found her and brought her back for further research."

"Why would they do that?" I asked.

"Because she was different. Not only did she look nothing like the other people in her village, but she had a rather unusual tattoo on her body. I'm sure you've seen it."

I said that I had.

"The tattoo has certain properties to it that are unlike anything even the Union has seen."

"Properties?"

She nodded. "You remember the chair she sat in, back in those ruins? Her tattoo activated the map in that place. It's how we were able to use it. It was the key."

"Her tattoo did that? How does that work?"

"No one knows for certain. It's believed to be tied directly to a certain technology."

"An ancient one," added Hitchens. "Specifically, the lost engineering of old Earth."

"The Union discovered Lex because of a rumor," continued Abigail. "It was said that a pod from space landed in a field, and that the farmer of that land discovered a baby inside, bearing a strange mark. When a pair of Union merchants came to trade, they heard the rumor and wanted to meet the little girl with the tattoo. They were shocked to see she was, in fact, alive and real. The news eventually reached the Union's science division, and it didn't take long for them to find Lex."

"We don't know if the Union has pieced together the connection between Lex's tattoo and Earth," said Fred. "They definitely understand there's something important about her."

"From what I saw in the labs, they seemed to be experimenting on her, trying to replicate the properties of the marking," said Abigail.

"What exactly is that tattoo?" I asked.

"Like I said, it's a key, but we don't know how and we don't know why," she answered. "All we know is that it works."

"In short, Captain," said Hitchens. "That little girl holds the key to finding Earth. It may be the only means we have of ever reaching it."

"If the Union ever gets their hands on her, they'll eventually figure out what we already know—that she has a connection to Earth. After that, they'll do everything in their power to extract whatever secrets are hidden in that tattoo, no matter the cost," said Abigail.

"What stopped them before?" I asked.

"The tattoo is actually organic and relies on Lex's own biology to function. The Union understands that if she dies, they lose the information," said Fred.

"They were working on a way to extract it when I took her," said Abigail. "I couldn't risk that happening, so I acted before we were ready. That's when things went wrong."

"You mean the senator," I said.

She nodded. "He was touring the facility when I made my escape. His men tried to stop us, but we managed to get through them. The senator was never part of the plan."

"When you say *we*, do you mean you and Lex?"

"There was another person helping me," said Abigail. "His name was Peter. He died on our way out. That was when the senator was killed, too. There was a firefight in one of the corridors. I protected Lex while Peter covered us."

"It's not your fault," said Fred.

I scoffed. "Sure it is. You ran in blind and botched the job. What did you think would happen?"

She looked at me, although there was no argument in her eyes. "You don't have to tell me."

The response took me by surprise. "So, you admit you messed up. That's good. Now you can learn from it and be better. You've got that kid to look after, so you can't screw up anymore."

She nodded.

After a brief silence, Freddie cleared his throat. "What are we going to do now, Captain? Do you have a plan?"

"I'm not taking you back to the church," I said, frankly. "But I won't leave you stranded, either."

Abigail lifted her eyes to look at me. "What do you mean?"

"You owe me a shitload of money, lady. All of you do. I expect you to find a way to pay, and quickly."

Hitchens, who had said very little until now, raised his finger. "I might have some extra credits."

"What's that?" I asked.

"The church recently sent me a nice sum for my research expenses. A grant of sorts."

"How much?" I asked.

"Ten thousand, I believe," he said, tapping his chin. "Would that be enough?"

"Not even close, but it's a start," I said. "Anyone else?"

"I don't have any money. I'm sure we can figure it out," said Fred.

"Good, because until we do, we're all in a world of shit. Maybe you didn't see the guy in charge of that small fleet. His name is Fratley, and he's ruthless. He'll torture and kill you all if he finds out you're on this boat."

"Let's avoid that outcome if we can," said Freddie.

"There might be a better way," mused Hitchens. "Tell me, Captain, do you know any traders who deal in relics or antiques?"

"I might know a guy," I said, immediately picturing Ollie, back on Taurus.

"If so, the solution might be right in front of us."

"How?" asked Fred.

"Do you recall the Cartographer on Epsilon?"

"How could I forget?" I asked. "Getting attacked by a bunch of wild animals is always memorable."

"Nevertheless, there are several points of interest there, aside from the ruins we visited. Octavia and I, along with other researchers at the church, have spent the last several years excavating that planet. We've uncovered several artifacts that we believe would net a small fortune."

"And where are these relics?" I asked.

"In a small facility, not far from Arcadia. I can give you the exact coordinates if you'd like."

"This isn't the kind of thing where one person thinks something is valuable, then it turns out to be a bunch of junk...is it?"

Hitchens waved his arms back and forth. "No, no, I assure you, these relics are quite valuable, Captain."

I considered the proposal. If he was right, it could mean getting Fratley off my back for good. If these relics turned out to be worthless, I might not have enough time to do another job. I'd be royally fucked.

"Okay," I finally said. "To hell with it. I didn't become a Renegade because it was easy. Let's see what you can do, Professor."

"I'm not a professor," corrected Hitchens.

"Whatever," I said. "Siggy, you listening?"

"As always," said Sigmond.

"Prime the engines. We've got a junkyard to loot." I let out my hand to Hitchens. "Now, let's hear those coordinates. There ain't much time to lose."

* * *

I thought about putting in a long-range request to speak with Ollie back on Taurus, but decided against it. The last thing I needed was someone catching the signal and listening in. They said the gal-net was secure, but I'd heard stories. There was talk that the Union had trackers in place to pick up on key words, and I couldn't risk getting found out before I delivered the goods. I'd have to take a chance on Ollie's ability to sell whatever I brought him. If the goods were decent, we wouldn't have a problem. I'd just have to wait to find out.

The facility Hitchens told me about was on a large asteroid in a system called DX192-9444-0. It was the kind of place you'd never visit, because there was almost nothing there. There was a single planet, sure, only it was a gas giant with liquid hydrogen oceans on its surface and little else. Hardly the kind of place you'd take a date.

According to the gal-net, it was theorized that there *used* to be another planet here, closer to the star, but it eventually exploded into an asteroid belt. Most believed it was due to a rogue comet hitting the planet. I got the impression none of them knew for sure.

Whatever the case, hardly a soul ever came this way. The belt had been mined and subsequently abandoned, just like so many other systems whose resources had been bled dry, and now it was ours.

"Our destination is one of the larger asteroids," said Sigmond as we entered the belt.

"Bring us in," I ordered.

"Shall I ready the shuttle for you, sir?"

"Sure, and while you're at it, tell Abigail and Freddie to meet me in the bay."

"As you wish," said the A.I.

I exited the cockpit and found Lex running around the outer ring of the lounge. She seemed to be playing and mumbling to herself, the way a kid does when they're in a world of their own. "Hey, Mr. Hughes, excuse me."

I stepped aside, letting her pass. "Careful," I told her. "If you trip and fall, I'm not cleaning you up."

"Sorry," she said.

"What's that in your hand?" I asked.

She showed me a small toy, some kind of tiny ship. "Abby gave it to me at the church. His name is Jerry."

"Jerry? What kind of name is that for a ship?"

"I dunno. That's just his name," she said, like she had nothing to do with it.

"Oh, well, why aren't you with someone? Did the nun get sick of you?"

She shook her head. "Abby's talking to the doctor. It was boring, so I left."

"Smart girl," I said. "All right, go on and play or whatever you were doing."

She smiled, then turned and resumed her nonsense.

Leaving the lounge, I quickly walked to the bay, where I found Freddie and Abigail waiting for me. To my surprise, Hitchens was also there. "I only need two of you. The doctor can wait in the lounge or his room."

"You'll need me to help locate the correct items," said Hitchens. "None of you know anything about my work."

"He has a point," said Abigail.

"That might be true, but you have to stay here."

"What for?" he asked.

"Because you don't have your own spacesuit, and you're too fat for mine," I said, rather bluntly.

Freddie's jaw dropped.

"Oh," muttered Hitchens. "I see. Well, that makes sense, I suppose."

"You can guide us from here. There's a camera on each of the suits that links directly to the ship's systems. Sigmond will set you up on the lounge's viewer."

"That's correct," said Sigmond, his voice booming from the overhead speaker.

"Ah, well, that makes things easier," said Hitchens, resting his hand on his side.

"As for you two, I hope you can handle a spacewalk. Suits are in that locker over there." I pointed behind them. "Gear up and let's get to it."

"W-Wait," said Fred. "I don't know if I can do that."

I paused. "Huh?"

"I've never gone on a real microgravity walk before."

"You what?" I asked.

"There's never been a reason for me to do something like that."

Even Abigail was surprised. "Didn't you take the training course? It's required on most Union worlds before you're allowed to fly."

"I'm from Shadderack. Our training program isn't what you'd call pristine."

"Shadderack?" asked Hitchens.

"It's a lesser known colony world. We don't utilize a lot of space travel, so most never have a reason to leave the planet. I only did because my education required—"

"Get to the point, Freddie," I said.

"Sorry. We mostly submerge ourselves in water for an hour, walk around, and that's it. The instructor signs off and we move on. The Union doesn't seem to mind it, since hardly anyone from Shadderack ever leaves the planet, let alone the solar system."

I went to the locker and pulled out a helmet. "Well, today you get some hands-on experience." I pushed the helmet into his arms. "It'll be a great learning exercise."

Fred looked down at the reflecting visor, spotting himself. "Oh, boy."

Abigail grabbed one of the suits from the locker and handed it to me. "Let's get this over with."

"That's the spirit," I said, grinning at the nun. "I like where your head's at."

# THIRTEEN

I stood on an asteroid, watching as my two companions departed the small shuttle.

Freddie nearly fell out of the vehicle, having had little experience with spacewalks before today. Still, he seemed to grasp the concept pretty quickly, once his feet were planted on the rock.

Abigail flicked on her suit's light, brightening the asteroid's surface.

I touched the side of the shuttle, detaching a flat piece of metal. It unfolded itself into a large, hovering cart with an extendable handle. This would make carrying the load back significantly easier once we located it.

Nearby, I spotted several discarded pieces of drilling machinery, most of which were likely inoperable. The gal-net had mentioned a mining operation taking place here some twenty years ago, making most of this equipment useless and archaic.

"Hitchens, you hearing me?" I asked, speaking through the com in my suit. "Give me a sign you're there."

"Is this thing on, Sigmond? Can he hear me?" asked the doctor.

"I can hear you," I acknowledged.

"I don't think he can hear me," said the archaeologist.

I couldn't help but roll my eyes. "Siggy, you got me?"

"Yes, sir," said the A.I.

"Tell Hitchens to shut up and tell us where to go."

"Oh, it's working now. Captain, this is Doctor Thadius Hitchens. Do you read me?"

"Yes."

"Excellent!" he exclaimed, cheerily. "Now, if you're all ready to go, I'm happy to lead you."

"Just get on with it," I said.

"You'll want to move through the area ahead of you. Do you see that rock over there? The one resembling a large eye? A short walk after that, you'll find the mine entrance. That's your destination."

"That's it?" I asked, surprised at how simple the directions were.

"Not quite. Once you're inside, the tunnel segments into several more. You'll want to follow my explicit directions if you are to reach the storage room."

"Did you two hear that?" I asked my companions.

"Loud and clear," said Abigail.

We both looked at Freddie, who seemed to be preoccupied with a green rock. "Fred?" I asked.

He looked up from the stone. "Oh, I'm sorry. I was just—"

"Were you even listening?" asked Abigail.

He got an embarrassed look on his face. "I'm so sorry."

"Just come on," I said, pushing the cart forward. "We've got work to do."

We passed by the stone Hitchens had mentioned, which I decided looked less like an eye and more like a testicle, although I kept the observation to myself.

A minute later, I spotted the mine in question. A feeble little cave that you'd only see if you were standing directly in front of it. The only signs of activity were the scattered drilling equipment, attached to the ground by hard wires, abandoned near the entrance.

"Okay, Doc, lead the way," I said over the com as we entered the cave. Before me was a long passage with several branching paths. It was too dark to see without turning on my helmet's light, which I decided to crank to the highest possible setting. The cave had no flat walls or floors. Instead, all sides were equally ridged.

"You'll need to disable your suit's gravity function," suggested Hitchens. "You can't walk this on foot."

"If I die in here, Hitchens, I'm coming for you," I warned, disabling the artificial gravity option. I lifted slightly off the ground, keeping my hand on the cart, which had its own mini-thrusters to allow for better control.

Abigail and Freddie did the same, each placing an arm on the cart's railing.

"Where to, Hitchens?" I finally asked.

"You'll want to take the first left, then right, then head straight...then pass two...no, *three* passages, and take the next left. Finally—"

"How about you tell us as we go," I suggested.

"Ah, yes. Sorry," he said. "Please, take the first left."

The three of us went forward, entering the cave and slowly making our way into the darkness. At the first break in the tunnel, I turned the cart into the second hall. We pressed on, with Hitchens guiding us through the labyrinth of corridors. I wasn't sure how the miners ever managed to get anything done in such an awful workspace. Unlike a moon or a planet, there was no north or south here, no true sense of direction. There was only forward and back, surrounded by the same stone on all sides. I felt like an insect, burying my way deep into the ground.

After several minutes, at the end of the final tunnel, we found an opening that lead into a sort of cavern. There were no doors to protect it, no barricades of any kind. As we drew closer, I could see there was nothing significant inside. I wondered if we'd taken a wrong turn somewhere.

Before I could say anything, Hitchens chimed in on the com, a satisfied tone in his voice. "Ah, now we're at it!"

"At what?" asked Freddie. "There's nothing here."

"Hardly so. This is only the foyer. There should be a panel on the far wall. Do you see it?"

Sure enough, there was a control panel hidden in the corner of the cave. It was difficult to see at first, being the same gray color as the rest of the wall. Freddie floated over to it and popped the cover open, revealing a number pad. "Got it," he said.

"Excellent," said Hitchens. "Next, you'll want to punch in the following: 6-6-4-2-9."

"You get that, Fred?" I asked.

"Not a problem," said the scholar.

He pressed the numbers, a hard click following each one, and then…

Nothing.

We stood there in silence, waiting for something to happen.

"Are you certain you did it correctly?" asked Abigail.

"6-6-4-2-9," said Freddie, repeating the code exactly as he'd heard it.

"Give it a moment," said Hitchens.

A second later, the nearby ground began to shake, and a wall cracked open, sliding up into the ceiling. "Here we go," said Fred.

"Aha!" exclaimed Hitchens. "Pardon the security measures. The wiring isn't exactly what you might call exemplary, though it is effective."

"Doesn't matter," I said, floating through the opening. "Let's get what we came for and head out."

The hidden area looked to hold a catalog of artifacts similar in design to what I saw on Epsilon. I had no idea if any of them were still operational, but it didn't matter. I was sure some rich asshole somewhere in the galaxy would pay their weight in credits to get their hands on this garbage.

Hell, if Ollie could sell ornaments he built out of old wiring he found in a dumpster, why not this?

As I entered into the final room, I felt a sudden weight on my body, and dropped to the ground, catching myself.

"Oh, goodness!" exclaimed Hitchens. "I should have mentioned, we installed artificial gravity in this section of the mine. Please be careful."

"Next time, how about you give us a warning first?" I asked, standing back up.

"My apologies," said Hitchens.

Crates and plastic-sealed machines filled the cave, delicately placed in perfect order. Fred accidentally bumped his foot into one as he entered, knocking it to the ground. I heard something shatter inside.

Abigail and I both looked at him, and I shook my head. "Really, Freddie?"

"I'm so sorry!" he said, trying to salvage the broken whatever-it-was.

"Will you be able to get the rest without breaking them?" asked Abigail. "Do you need to wait outside?"

"No, I promise I'll be more careful, Sister."

I chuckled. "You're getting lectured."

The nun turned and glared at me.

"Don't try that shit on me," I told her, shutting her down before she could start. "I'll leave your ass stranded."

"A word of warning, Captain," said Hitchens. "You'll want to be especially careful with the cargo marked with a yellow indicator. Those are particularly fragile, and therefore more valuable."

I saw Freddie checking the box he'd broken. He frowned at the yellow marker.

I shook my head again. "Poor, poor Freddie."

We loaded what we could on the cart and began our way back toward the entrance. The path out was a little easier, although I don't know what we would have done without Hitchens guiding us. Considering how much cargo we still had to retrieve from that cave, we were looking at several more trips, but I was certain we'd be done before the day was through.

Thankfully, loading the crates into the back of the shuttle was significantly easier than it was in the cave. I lifted a box with one hand, which had previously required both Freddie and I to move.

We filled the shuttle in no time, then returned to the mine. It was easy-going for a while. It even began to feel routine. Walk through the mine, load the cart, walk back to the shuttle, load it up. Repeat.

We managed to take a shuttle's worth of artifacts up to The Star, store them in the cargo bay, then return for another load.

It wasn't until a few hours later that everything went to total and complete shit.

* * *

"Sir," began Sigmond as we loaded another cart full of equipment. "I'm detecting something."

I stopped what I was doing. "What is it, Siggy?"

"A slip tunnel has appeared in this system. I believe another ship has entered the area."

"Another ship? Can you see who it is?"

"I'm afraid not. Shall I raise the cloak?"

"Do it," I ordered. "We're on our way back. Expect the shuttle in a few."

"What's wrong?" asked Abigail.

"Sounds like we've got company. Come on, we've gotta go."

"What about the rest of—"

"Leave it. We've got enough. Let's get back to *The Star*," I said, beginning to do just that.

We moved as fast as we could through the tunnels, but the lack of gravity made for slow progress.

After we reached the shuttle, I had the two of them board and get strapped in. I hit the com, closing my door and starting the engines. "Siggy, we're heading back. Get ready to punch it as soon as we're onboard."

The shuttle lifted off of the asteroid, hovering for a second before finally taking off. We maneuvered through the belt, bypassing several hulking rocks that could have easily crushed us.

"We're nearly there," I told the others.

"Sir, be cautious," warned Sigmond. "The other ship is moving closer to your position. They do not seem to be aware of us, but—"

At that moment, I felt the shuttle rattle violently as a torpedo nearly struck our side.

It blasted a chunk of rock from an asteroid, shattering the stone and sending us into a spin. "What the fuck!" I yelled as we began our descent back toward the same rock we'd only just left.

I hit the stabilizer and took manual control, trying my best to steady the ship. It nearly worked, but there wasn't enough time. Instead of leveling out, we hit the surface and slid four dozen meters until we slammed straight into a small cliff.

The sides of the doors and the dash released a white puffy material, shielding our bodies from most of the impact.

Freddie screamed, hitting his head against Abigail's seat. I could already see the blood from his nose.

When the commotion finally stopped, I looked at Abigail. "Are you okay?"

She was breathing quickly, confusion still in her eyes.

"Hey, Abby. Look at me." I put my hand on her arm. "Focus on what I'm saying. Look at me. Hey!"

She turned and tried to focus on my face. Her eyes were

swirling. "What...happened?"

"Hold on." I reached beneath the dash and took out a small red medical box. I took the scanner inside and activated it, running the device along her head and chest, checking for any signs of damage or swelling.

Fred kept his head up and elevated, covering his bleeding nose with his hand. I grabbed his hand. "Let it bleed, you idiot!" I barked. "You'll give yourself a pulmonary embolism that way!"

"S-Sorry. Is Sister Abigail okay?" he asked, apparently more concerned with her than himself.

"It looks like she has some bruising, but nothing's broken," I said, closing the scanner. "Abby, are you with us?"

The disconnected look in her eyes was finally gone. She blinked several times, staring back at me. "I-I'm here. I'm okay."

"Godsdammit," I said, punching the seat. "Who are these bastards? I'll have Siggy fire a hole clean through their—"

"Attention intruders," said a voice over the com. It sounded like an automated message. "You are encroaching on Sarkonian territory. Prepare to surrender your vessel."

"Who are the Sarkonians?" asked Fred.

I tapped the com. "Who the hell is this? I want to speak to your representative right now."

"Please prepare to surrender your vessel," repeated the voice.

I cursed and hit the seat again. Next to Fratley, Sarkonians were probably the last thing I wanted to deal with right now. They liked to confiscate ships and property that they felt were in their territory, but since Sarkonians had no defined borders, their claims were impossible to predict. The rule of thumb in the Deadlands was, if you saw a Sarkonian ship, you turned and ran away as fast as you damn well could.

"Siggy, scan that ship and tell me what we're dealing with."

"Are we in trouble?" asked Freddie.

I raised my finger to quiet him. "Not if I can help it."

"I'm detecting one quad cannon, and only a second-grade hull," said Sigmond.

Freddie pulled the cloth away from his nose. "Is that bad?"

"Only for them," I said, kicking open the door. "Siggy, get ready to blow that piece of shit out of the sky, you hear me?"

"I do, sir," said the A.I.

I got to my feet and stared into the asteroid belt at the oncoming Sarkonian vessel. "Time to show these assholes why you should never fuck with a Renegade."

* * *

Standing with my pistol in one hand, I waved at the enemy ship. "That's right, you jackasses. Come right over here."

As the Sarkonian ship neared us, they opened their bay door. An unmanned shuttle exited and began making its way towards us. No doubt, if they had their way, we'd wind up working in an ore mine by the end of the day.

Too bad Siggy and I had other plans.

Before the shuttle could get more than a hundred meters from the Sarkonian vessel, *The Renegade Star* decloaked from beneath another large asteroid, firing at the enemy ship.

The quad-cannons unleashed a string of rapid-fire shots, taking them by surprise. The ship withstood the many hits, much to my own surprise, and returned fire at *The Star*. Thanks to Siggy's inhuman reaction speed, he managed to maneuver behind another asteroid, allowing the rock to shield most of the damage.

Chunks of stone broke apart, scattering in every direction, including towards us. "Get out of the shuttle!" I ordered, reaching my arm inside and grabbing Abigail by the hand.

She and Fred stumbled out of the door, scurrying on the hard surface of the asteroid and together we attempted to flee, back towards the mine.

Three large ship-sized rocks spiraled towards us, smashing into the ground and, incidentally, crushing our shuttle. I cursed under my breath at the loss. Those things were expensive and on top of all the other debt I had, this would only add to it.

I pushed the thought out of my head and decided to be pissed later. For now, I ran, hoping I didn't trip and rip my damn suit in the process.

As we reached the giant eye-shaped monument near the mine, I called for Sigmond to fire a second wave.

He did, and the missiles hit the Sarkonian ship right in the same spot they had before, puncturing their deck and sending pieces of cargo into space. I watched the entire event unfold on my visor as Siggy broadcasted it to me.

The enemy vessel opened a slip tunnel, attempting to flee, and I gave the order to fire one last volley.

Sigmond did as I said, sending a final wave of six missiles towards the enemy ship. Two collided with a cluster of smaller asteroids, but the remaining four managed to get through.

The Sarkonian vessel could do nothing to stop the barrage from penetrating their hull, obliterating the ship from the inside. The vessel splintered, exploding into a cloud of wreckage, scattering in all directions.

"Oh, my gods," muttered Fred, gawking at the obliterated ship.

I looked at Abigail, who was watching the whole mess unfold. "You good?" I asked.

She still looked dazed, albeit a little less than before. "I just want to get out of here."

"Sounds like my kind of plan," I said.

I could have ordered them to keep working, maybe try to salvage the artifacts in the destroyed shuttle, but we had enough cargo onboard *The Star* to call this a success. There was no use chancing another Sarkonian attack.

The ship came down through the asteroid field, rising above us, hovering momentarily. "Are you ready to depart, sir?" asked

Sigmond.

"Can it land?" asked Fred.

"There's no solid surface wide enough, but I'm sure Siggy can make it work."

"Stand clear," said the A.I.

I waved the others back as the ship approached, stopping a few meters from the surface.

"Bring it closer," I ordered.

"Not possible," Sigmond replied.

The base of the ship was a short distance above us, not close enough to reach by hand. We'd have to float up to reach it.

I waved at Abigail and Freddie to join me. "Time to go," I said, pointing to the ship.

They both looked up at the cargo lift door. "I take it we're supposed to jump," said Freddie.

"And hope you make it," I added, clasping my hands together. "Come on, I'll give you a boost."

Freddie placed his foot between my fingers, and I pushed him up, watching as he floated towards the door. He waved his arms around, frantically, before finally catching the base of the lift. "I have it!"

I breathed a sigh of relief, then looked at Abigail. "You're up next."

"I can manage," she assured me, squatting to the ground. She took a slow, deep breath, and jumped.

I watched her confidently sail towards the ship, perfectly aimed. She reached it easily, grabbing the railing with her whole arm, attempting to swing herself around. As she did, she seemed to react, partially losing her grip.

Freddie reached for her, taking Abigail's hand and pulling her onto the deck. "I have you!"

"What's wrong?" I asked.

I could hear her breathing heavily. "Nothing, it's just..." Her voice trailed off. "Sorry, my shoulder was hurting. It's fine now."

"Must have been from the crash," I said.

"Are you ready, Captain?" asked Freddie.

I crouched, placing both my hands on the rock beneath me, then pushed my feet down, extending my body and launching myself straight up towards *The Star.*

I nearly passed the opening as I floated, but a hand grasped at me, yanking me back. "Got you!" said Abigail. She held me tight, squeezing my fingers.

Fred took my wrist as well, and together the two of them pulled me inside. As I entered the cargo deck, the ship's artificial gravity took hold and brought me straight down on my ass, knocking both Abigail and Fred on their sides.

"Welcome back, sir," Sigmond said inside my ear as the lift began to close shut. "Shall I chart a course to Taurus Station?"

"I think that'd be a fine idea, Siggy," I said, feeling a sudden ache in my lower back.

Fred ran over and offered his hand. "Now what?"

"Now nothing," I said, then waited for the oxygen to fill the cargo bay. Once the doors were sealed, I removed my helmet and took a long breath. "The shuttle's gone and we have our cargo. I think we've done enough for one day, don't you?"

# FOURTEEN

After a long, hard sleep and a cup of coffee, I went to check on Abigail. She needed more medical attention than I thought. The scanner I used had missed the concussion, which wasn't a surprise. I found that thing in a pawn shop over a year ago, but never had to use it. Go figure it barely worked.

I found her with Octavia, who had a decent bit of experience with patching wounds, as it turned out. "How's she looking?" I asked when the door opened.

Octavia motioned at the sleeping woman in her bed. "She's resting, but she'll be fine."

"How'd you learn how to handle that?"

"I used to be in the Union Guard," she explained.

"You?" I asked.

"I wasn't always Dr. Hitchens' assistant. In my other life, I was a patriot."

"Is that what they call dogs of the military where you come from?"

My bluntness didn't faze her, or if it did, she didn't let it show. "The Union isn't cruel to every world, Mr. Hughes," she said. "I was born on Androsia."

Androsia was the capital of the Union, so I knew the name, despite never stepping foot on its soil. "Boy, talk about a silver spoon," I said. "That must have been an easy life for you."

"It was," she admitted. "I used to think the whole Empire was like that. I thought everyone was happy. It wasn't until I saw the outer colonies with my own eyes that I began to understand."

"I'm not sure if I should be happy for you or not," I said. "Seems like you gave up a lot just to be someone's assistant."

She nodded. "I suppose I did. My father was a surgeon on the richest planet in the Union. We had enough money to last a lifetime. But living an easy life isn't the same as being fulfilled. It doesn't mean you'll be happy. I gave it up because I felt a need for something more. I wanted to study history, to explore."

"You felt confined," I said.

"Living in the capitol, I had my entire life planned out. I was to do my duty and serve the Union, then go to medical school like my father. No one asked me what I wanted. It was like living in a really comfortable box where all your needs are met, except you can never leave. For most people, that's enough. For me, it felt claustrophobic. You seem like you understand that."

"I might," I said, refusing to elaborate. "How long before the nun recovers?"

The sudden question didn't throw her. She leaned back, looking at Abigail's bed. "Miss Pryar needs to rest a while. Give her a day."

"Thanks for handling it. I've got enough to do as it is."

She gave me a slight smile. "I'm sure you do, Captain."

I started to ask what she meant, only to drop it and return to the lounge.

I kept mulling over our haul from the asteroid. I had no idea if it was worth anything, but with some much-needed luck, Ollie might be able to find me a buyer. Probably a sucker on the prowl for antiques. I just hoped we'd get enough to cover the debt.

In the lounge, Hitchens sat with Freddie and Lex, watching one of the old Foxy Stardust cartoons. I took a seat and didn't say anything. Lex had a wide-eyed expression on her face, totally engrossed in the show. Hitchens was on his pad, reading an article, while Freddie just sat there, eating an apple.

It would be strange, once this job was done, to return to such a quiet ship. It wouldn't be the first time I'd carried so many passengers, but this mission had certainly lasted longer than most.

I expected them all to leave once we arrived at the station. No doubt, they'd try to charter a new ship, one with a less dangerous captain at its helm. I was in over my head with Fratley, and after the shocking display back at Arcadia, I was sure they'd want to avoid the bastard at all costs.

Whatever they ended up doing, I hoped they didn't get themselves killed.

"Excuse me, sir," said Sigmond, speaking in my ear. "Please report to the cockpit. There's something you need to see."

"What is it, Siggy?" I asked, surprised that he wasn't speaking through the speaker.

"We may have a problem."

I casually took my leave of the room and headed to the front of the ship, saying nothing. After closing the door to the hall, I took a seat.

A few moments ago, *The Star* had come out of a slip tunnel, so the space outside the ship was still and quiet, glowing dots in the distance. No sign of trouble. "What's the deal? You see something I don't?"

"I'm detecting a Union star cruiser near the other end of the next slip tunnel, sir. I believe they are entering soon."

I blinked. "A cruiser? And they're heading here?"

"Yes, I believe so."

A series of questions hit me all at once. Could they be looking for us? Had the Union discovered our location and found a way to track the girl or my ship? Was it some new directive, as part of their recent border expansion program? I'd heard rumors about them going into the Deadlands a handful of times, but that was so rare. They generally kept to their own space.

Could Lex really be so important to them?

I hoped I was overthinking it, and this was something unrelated. With any luck, we'd pass each other in the tunnel, off to our own destinations. Scans didn't work in slipspace, so if the cruiser continued on its course, we'd have nothing to worry about. The only concern was whether they had a means of penetrating our cloak. We could see them from here with our long-range sensors, which normally would mean the same for them, but only if they had a means of detecting the cloak. If not, then we just might be able to make it through without any trouble.

"They're entering the tunnel," said Sigmond.

"How long?" I asked.

"They will reach our present location in approximately three hours."

"Enter the tunnel as soon as they do. Wait until the cruiser is fully inside. We don't want them to see us when we drop our cloak."

"Actually, sir, it may not be that simple."

"Why is that?"

"If we enter at the same time as the cruiser, we'll most likely leave at the same time. If anything, they will emerge slightly before us. If that happens, we won't be cloaked in time to shield ourselves."

I knew he was right and cursed myself for not realizing it sooner. If we entered the tunnel now, the cruiser would emerge before us. All they'd have to do is scan behind them to see us coming out the same point they entered. Even if we waited an hour or two, there was still a risk that they'd see us when we emerged.

"We could remain cloaked in this position and wait," suggested Sigmond.

"No, there's gotta be another way that doesn't involve us waiting here for a cruiser to arrive. I don't want to risk them detecting us through the cloak." I flicked the side of my chair, weighing the options. There were other tunnels running through here, certainly, and we could take any of them we wanted, but the detour would prolong our arrival at Taurus, possibly by a day or more. "Siggy, what if we stay on this tunnel until we're out of scanning range? Where would we come out?"

"That would bring us inside Union-controlled space."

"Would we be near anything? Any planets or colonies? Space stations?"

"None, according to the galactic map."

"How long to return to Taurus with only standard warp thrusters?" I asked.

"Six hours," Sigmond said.

"And if we use one of the other tunnels nearby? How long would that take?"

"There are three tunnels besides this one, but the detour would add another three days to our travel time."

I thought about Abigail in her bed, knowing she needed better treatment than what my ship could provide. If we waited too long, she might end up suffering. "Fuck it, let's take this tunnel and bypass Taurus. Once we get there, cloak us and turn around."

"Right away, sir."

A beam from our ship split a tear in space, opening to reveal the jade-colored lights of slipspace. "In we go," I said, leaning back in my chair.

Our cloak dropped and *The Renegade Star* pushed into the rift.

At the same time, the Union cruiser was on its way to our location, flying in the opposite direction through slipspace. We would pass each other soon, unaware of the other's presence.

Entering Union space wasn't the most ideal scenario, I had to admit, but it was better than waiting three days to return to Taurus Station. Aside from Abigail's health, there was also the matter of our cargo, which had to be sold so I could pay Fratley back before the end of the week.

The deadline was fast approaching, and I couldn't risk bringing Fratley's wrath down on me. One way or the other, I had to get that bastard his money.

# FIFTEEN

I made it a point to avoid Union space, whenever possible. I'd crossed the border when I had to, depending on the job, but there were always certain risks involved. Risks that generally outweighed the dangers of operating within the Deadlands.

Sure, the Deadlands had ravagers, thieves, pirates, and Sarkonians, but at least I never had to deal with Union checkpoints or military envoys. While I could always handle a few small pirate ships, the Union controlled the largest and most powerful armada in the galaxy. That was the kind of trouble you just didn't want.

Union space also had several long-range buoys to monitor border activity. If one of them caught a glimpse of you, there was a chance you'd end up having a rough time. I even had to watch where and how I used my cloak, since the technology was illegal here.

And now I was back, perhaps to my own detriment. Fratley needed his money, and I needed to live, which meant I didn't have the luxury of being cautious.

"We will arrive at Taurus Station in approximately six hours,"

Sigmond told me as we raised the cloak and set out from the slip tunnel.

"Keep your eyes out for any sign of Union activity," I said. "I don't want us anywhere near one of their ships."

"I will adjust our route, should the situation call for it."

"Good man," I said, sitting in my bed.

I hadn't bothered telling the others about the cruiser we spotted near the tunnel. There was no need for them to know that the Union was inside the Deadlands. Maybe I'd inform them later, but with everything that had happened to the church, to Abigail, and to all of us, I knew they didn't need to know. Not right now.

My head swirled in a fog as I sat on the bed. I'd been increasingly exhausted these last few days, a testament to how overworked I was, most likely.

I leaned back in my bunk and felt the soft embrace of my pillow, falling straight to sleep as soon as my eyes closed.

When I opened my eyes, I felt a stiffness in my jaw, and sat up. Glancing at my pad, I saw we were nearly at our destination. Half an hour more. Five and a half hours had gone by in a blink.

I yawned. "Siggy, put me through to our guests, would you?"

"Right away, sir," he confirmed. "Speak when you're ready."

I cleared my throat, wiping the grime from my eyes. "Everyone, we'll be at Taurus in a few," I announced, and I heard my voice over the coms outside my room. "Pack your shit and standby."

Elegantly put," remarked Sigmond.

I threw a shirt on and cracked my back, then took a drink from my water jug. As I stood, I heard something against my door. It wasn't quite a knock. More like a light tap.

I opened it and looked down to see Lex standing alone in front of me.

"Mr. Hughes, you sleep too much," said the little albino.

"What do you want, kid?"

"I'm hungry and there's no more food."

"We're out already?"

I went to the food dispenser and opened all the cabinets, finding most of it empty. There were a few pieces of jerky, but not much else to speak of. "Damn, you people cleaned me out."

"Can I have something, please?" asked Lex. "My stomach hurts."

I offered her a piece of jerky. "Eat up."

She smelled it and, twisting her nose, quickly shoved it back in my hand. "Gross!"

I bit into it, munching on the processed meat. "What's wrong? Not a fan of jerky?"

"It smells like butt."

"What? You don't like butts?" I asked, taking a whiff of the meat.

She giggled at my joke. "Ew."

"Tell you what," I said, taking a piece of candy from my side pocket. "Eat half a stick of jerky and you can have a sweet. What do you say, kid?"

Her eyes widened at the sight of the treat. "I can have that?"

"You just gotta eat the other thing first."

She looked at the meat, then back at the candy. "Um."

I stuck out my hand with the jerky. "Here."

She took it, a little reluctantly. With her eyes on the candy, she bit into the meat, chewing slowly.

"Well?" I asked, watching her make what I was certain was the ultimate sacrifice.

She seemed to relax as she continued to eat. "It's okay," she said, swallowing and taking another bite. She looked up at me. "Still not good, though."

I laughed. "Here you go, kid." I tossed the candy and she caught it, the jerky hanging out of her mouth.

"Wow!" she exclaimed.

"Eat the jerky first, then you can have the candy. Got it?"

She nodded. "Thanks, Mr. Hughes!"

I left with the second piece of jerky, eating it while I made my way to the hangar bay. Lex followed after me, munching on her own food as fast as she could. By the time we reached the end of the hall, she was unwrapping the candy, a giddy expression on her face.

Hitchens had been spending a fair amount of time in the cargo bay since we left the asteroid belt. I had, before now, left him to do his work in peace, but we were drawing close to the station now and I wanted to make sure our cargo was fully intact.

"Ah, Captain Hughes," said the doctor as I made my way down the steps. He had several of the relics we'd found in the mine placed neatly around the floor. Each one had an piece of paper attached to it with an identification number written on it, most likely to help keep track of the inventory.

"Looks like you're staying busy," I said, looking at one of the machines. Its tag read 021.

"I've been organizing our collection," he explained.

"Which of these are you keeping and which are we selling?"

"Items one through eight are to remain in my possession."

"How high does the list go?"

"Forty-six," he said. "Not quite the catalog we once had, though it remains a respectable collection."

I did the math in my head. "So, we're selling...thirty-seven?"

"Thirty-eight," he corrected, an always-respectful tone in his voice.

"I kept meaning to ask, why did you have all this shit stored in that mine in the first place?"

"The Council saw the need to keep our findings hidden, should the Union or another party such as that Fratley fellow ever see fit to invade Arcadia. I was opposed to the notion originally, yet it seems the Council was correct to insist upon it. Loralin, specifically, if memory serves." He wiped some sweat from his brow with a small, red handkerchief, then paused for several seconds, like he was lost in thought.

"Doc, are you okay?" I asked, snapping my fingers.

He blinked. "Oh, I apologize, Captain. I was thinking about them again. Our friends in the Church. They're still heavy on my mind, it seems." He cleared his throat. "Anyway, as I was saying, the technology itself was something of a mystery when we first discovered it. We had little information about what each of these machines actually did."

"And now?" I asked, looking at the dozens of devices scattered neatly across my ship's floor.

"Sadly, most are inactive," he explained. "The only exceptions are the eight I mentioned before."

"That one's my favorite," said Lex. Her voice caught me off guard. I'd forgotten she was even there. She pointed to a small box in the corner, near Hitchens.

"Ah, yes. Such an exquisite find," he said.

Lex ran to it and picked it up. As she touched it, I was surprised to see it brighten, a small light emanating from its surface, followed by a soft, melodic series of tones.

Lex smiled, giggling at the sounds. "Isn't it pretty?"

I listened, intently, but couldn't recognize the song, if that's what it truly was.

"Lex has been assisting me," said Hitchens.

I put out my hand to Lex. "Can I see that?"

She smiled and gave me the box. The second it left her hand, the music stopped and the light grew dim and empty.

"As you can see, Lex's mark allows her to interact with each of these objects. It's quite remarkable."

"You're talking about her tattoo," I said, glancing at the blue lines on her neck. An image of Lex sitting in the mysterious chair inside the cave swept through my mind.

"Exactly right, Captain. The mark gives her the ability to activate each and every one of these machines. Why that is, I don't fully understand, but her very proximity is often enough to bring them online."

I still had trouble believing that the girl could do what he was suggesting. Since when did a tattoo give someone the ability to activate anything? Most of the time, they were just an eyesore.

Even if it was true, who would give such a valuable thing to a little kid?

"Some don't work, though," said Lex, frowning. She pointed to the other machines.

"Indeed. Only the eight are operational, and I had to replace several parts in each to get them working."

"You fixed them?" I asked, handing the box back to Lex.

She took it and the music started up again, and she smiled.

"Thankfully, yes," said Hitchens. "I was able to salvage pieces from a few of them to fix these eight. This technology is nearly two thousand years old, so most of them had at least one broken part.

I'm actually surprised I was able to get any of them to work in the first place."

"What about the map you found? How did you know it would work if it was so old? Did you know it would work before we went all the way out there?"

He let out a short laugh. "Heavens no, Captain. I wasn't even certain Lex existed until Sister Abigail brought her back. For that matter, putting her in that chair was only a theory."

"A theory?" I asked.

He nodded. "I didn't have time to perform any tests on her before we left. The only information we had came from the notes we stole from that Union lab. When you and Ms. Pryar arrived, the rest of us had to move quickly."

I looked at Lex, who was humming along with the machine, bouncing from one foot to the other. She walked to the stairs at the back of the bay and sat down. "That's quite a gamble you took," I said, turning back to him.

"You have to understand. Lex is unique. Part of her tattoo resembles the emblem on the Cartographer, so we knew there had to be a connection."

"You had to know they'd come after her," I said.

"We did," said Hitchens. "Frankly, we were fortunate to get the child home when we did."

"And you really think that map you found leads to Earth?"

"I wouldn't be risking my life and career if I didn't."

"Well, for what it's worth, Doc, I hope you're right."

"Thank you, Captain. That means a great deal, considering your doubts."

"I may find the whole thing ridiculous, but that doesn't mean I don't want it to be true."

"I appreciate your skepticism," said the doctor, a slight smile on his face. Perhaps one day you'll have the proof you need to believe."

I laughed. "Now, wouldn't that be something?"

\* \* \*

We arrived at Taurus and had to wait in line over an hour before they let us dock. A bit unusual in my experience.

Sigmond brought the ship in once we got the go-ahead, and I felt a sweeping relief wash over me as the station locked its docking clamp around *The Renegade Star's* airlock.

I met everyone in the hall. They each had their bags in hand and ready to disembark. I could see the eagerness on a few of their faces. After days in a cramped ship, they had to be ready for something with a little more area to it. Maybe a room with a raised ceiling, such as the promenade.

"Everyone ready?" I asked, tapping in my access code to open the airlock.

Abigail stood next to Lex and Octavia. She looked better than before, much less dazed, but still tired.

I gave her a nod and she returned it.

The door slid up and a cold breeze hit us, sweeping through the inner hall of my ship. It felt refreshing, just like every other visit. The fresh air conditioning reminded me that I needed to replace the one on *The Star*.

Freddie reached out his hand. "Thank you for the safe journey, Captain."

I shook it. "Not a problem."

"We'll be at the hotel on deck 4. I'll be using my name, so ask for Tabernacle."

"Taber-what?"

"Tabernacle. That's my last name."

I raised my eye at him. "Since when?"

He laughed and shook his head, like I'd said a joke, then walked through the door and into the station.

Everyone followed, disembarking the ship. As most of them continued toward the promenade, Hitchens paused at my side, along with Octavia. "Captain, shall we accompany you to see your man?"

"My man?" I asked.

He looked around, even though no one was there, and leaned in. He covered the side of his mouth and whispered, "You know...*the dealer*."

I pushed his hand away. "His name is Ollie, and sure, you can come if you want. Try to relax, though. This isn't a spy movie."

He clasped his hands together. "Oh, wonderful!" he exclaimed as we began to walk down the platform. "This will be so exciting."

The promenade was less congested than I expected, especially during this time of day. Typically, there was a decent-sized crowd gathering around the shops and bars. Travelers, mostly, and tourists. It made it easy for people like myself to blend in.

Ollie's shop wasn't far from where we pulled in. I knew he'd be there, too, since the poor schmuck never took a day off. Whatever he was, Ollie was reliable.

"Jace!" he yelled when he saw me coming.

I nodded at him. "Ollie. Good to see you."

"You've been gone a bit longer than I expected. What happened with that job? You know, the one with the nun. I'm still waiting on my cut, by the way. When are you gonna pay me?"

"It got complicated," I said, approaching the counter. "Haven't had time to send the money yet, but I'll take care of it after this."

"Yeah, you better, pal," he said. Ollie had one of his suits on today. Turquoise blue with a little gold trim. Not exactly my kind of thing, although somehow it worked for him. "You ought to bring me something nice when you stay away for so long."

"You're the one who sells cheap souvenirs. I figured you had enough to last a lifetime."

"I'll have you know, my goods make the best gifts on the station. Ask anyone who shops here. Anyway, who are your friends?" asked Ollie.

"His name is Hitchens," I explained. "He's a professor. This is his assistant, Octavia"

"A doctor of archaeology, actually. Not a professor," corrected Hitchens.

I shrugged. "Doesn't matter. He's here to help explain the cargo I need to sell, in case you have questions."

"Cargo?" asked Ollie.

"We picked up some old tech. I think it's pre-Union. Since you're in the market of selling useless shit to rich idiots, I thought you'd be the guy to talk to."

"Damn, and this whole time I thought you were stopping by because you missed my face."

"The catalogue includes over three dozen items," said Hitchens.

"I'll have to take a look before I say for sure. Did you bring anything with you?"

Hitchens opened his satchel and set a small metallic object on the countertop. It was bronze and circular, interwoven with beautiful designs. The carvings, I noticed, were remarkably similar to Lex's tattoo.

Ollie's eyes widened at the sight of the machine. "Oh, well, look at that."

"This particular artifact is, by my estimates, 1300 years old," said Hitchens.

Ollie took out a small device, which could only be a scanner, and waved it along the relic. A light blinked, and Ollie grinned. "Oh, yes. Yes, yes, yes." He looked up at me. "Jace, you always bring me the best stuff."

"Glad you like it," I said.

"Higgins, is the rest of your supply like this?" asked Ollie.

"It's *Hitchens*," corrected the doctor. "To answer your question, it most certainly is."

Ollie's eyebrows shot up. "Oh yeah, Jace. I can sell this for sure. Let's go get the rest and I'll set up a meeting with some buyers first thing tomorrow morning. I'll be needing the usual 10% to cover my fee, naturally."

"How much do you think you can get?" I asked.

"If the rest of the merchandise is like this? I'd say you could be looking at a hundred thousand, easy."

I blinked. "Seriously? A hundred thousand for a bunch of machines?"

Ollie laughed. "Look around this shop," he said, waving his hand at the array of tiny trinkets, made primarily with discarded junk. "You should know by now that people will buy just about anything if you tell them it's worth something."

"These machines are valuable," insisted Hitchens.

"It's garbage," said Ollie. "And it's old as shit, which means it's valuable."

Hitchens dropped his mouth like he was insulted. "But—"

"Let it go, Doc," I said, touching his shoulder. "Ollie can call our cargo garbage all he wants, so long as he delivers the right payment."

"Trust me," said Ollie with the same bravado I'd witnessed so many times before. "No one knows this business better than me."

* * *

Ollie, Octavia, and I moved the thirty-eight artifacts from my cargo bay and unloaded them into the back room of the shop. He was eager to start making calls to his associates, so the rest of us agreed to give him some space.

"Call me in the morning," Ollie said.

"That's a fast turnaround. You sure you don't need more time?"

"There's always someone eager to get their hands on this stuff. Trust me. I see postings for it all the time."

"Great. Thanks again, Ollie," I said, tapping his shoulder.

"Anytime, Jace. Just do me a favor, would you?"

"What is it?" I asked.

Ollie leaned in. "That girl you're with. The assistant to the fat guy. Think you could put a good word in for me?"

"You mean Octavia?"

"Yeah, she's a looker, that one."

"I'll see what I can do," I said, glancing back at Octavia, who was standing at the entrance to the shop with Hitchens.

Ollie's eyes lit up. "Really? Damn, Jace, you're a good pal."

"Just sell my stuff and we'll call it even," I said, turning to leave. "See you tomorrow."

I said goodbye to Hitchens and Octavia, who went to join their friends in the hotel on floor twelve. They'd join me on the promenade first thing tomorrow so we could meet back up with Ollie. Until then, everyone was free to relax.

I thought about heading to the bar, ultimately opting to just go to my room and crash for the night. It was early, sure, but I didn't operate on a typical sleep schedule. That was for people with day jobs. People who sat in a cubicle or an office and performed a mindless task for eight hours a day. Me? I didn't have the luxury of going home at the end of a shift and clocking out. My job didn't end, which meant that sometimes I couldn't rest.

Not that I was complaining. This was the life I'd chosen, and it was a good one. A lawless one, full of freedom and open space. The last thing I wanted was to be trapped in a room, behind a computer screen, logging data-entry points and reading memos.

I'd fought tooth and nail to get to where I was, including taking out that loan from Fratley. All I had to do was pay him off and then I'd be free to do as I pleased. No more debt to struggle with, no more asshole breathing down my neck.

I thought about the money I was about to make, thanks to Ollie and those artifact machines. While I was still thinking about it, I went ahead and transferred ten percent of my earnings from the last job into Ollie's account. Fair was fair, after all.

*Almost there*, I thought as I closed my eyes to sleep. *I'll fix the rest tomorrow.*

# SIXTEEN

A few minutes after I woke, I noticed my pad blinking an alert. Ollie had mentioned calling me, so my only guess was that I missed it while I was asleep.

I swiped the screen and saw a video recording in my inbox. As expected, it was signed Ollie Trinidad.

I tapped the name and Ollie's face filled the screen.

"Jace, it's me. I guess you're still asleep, so listen up. I called and got a deal with a buyer. They've transferred the money directly into my account, so I'm sending your share straight to you. Enjoy, pal. Just stop by sometime after lunch and we'll celebrate. The buyer is on his way now to pick up the goods. Anyway, see ya soon."

I quickly pulled up my bank account, using the gal-net. After logging in, I was shocked to see a whopping one hundred and ten thousand credits sitting there. Talk about a beautiful sight. I swear, I could have cried.

The video ended with a timestamp, suggesting it had been sent in the early morning, around 0600. I checked the clock and saw it was currently 0900. Boy, had I slept late.

Was it really over? All that work to get this money, but it was finally done. I had the payment and Fratley could be satisfied. I could take my ship and go anywhere, do anything I wanted.

I slammed my fist into my mattress, smiling as I stared at the number in my account.

After a quick stretch, I got up and showered, taking my time. There was no need to rush anymore.

It wasn't noon yet, so I decided I wanted to catch a glimpse of these buyers, if possible, and see who was actually willing to shell out so many creds for a bunch of useless toys. Then, I'd buy Ollie a drink to show him my thanks. The little weasel really came through for me, same as always.

When I was in the hall, leaving my room, I called Sigmond and asked him to tell Hitchens to meet me on the Promenade. The jolly researcher was more than eager to do so, giving me a warm acknowledgement.

I stopped in at the bar, briefly, for a cup of their terrible coffee, giving my salute to the same bartender I'd met the last time I was here. "Thanks," I told him, taking the cup from the counter.

"No problem. You in dock for long?" he asked.

"I aim to leave today, actually." I took a sip and was surprised at how good it tasted. The coffee on my ship was usually the best, but this blend wasn't much worse.

"I can't say I blame you," said the barkeep. "There's some sketchy people here today. Moreso than usual."

"Sketchy?" I asked. "We get another group of ravagers in?"

"Nah, more like military guys. I saw some uniforms heading upstairs."

"Military? You're sure?"

He nodded. "Seemed like it. I didn't get a good look, but someone mentioned they were with the Union. I don't believe it, though. Ain't seen any Union guys around here in over a year."

That wasn't good. The last thing I needed to deal with was the military snooping around. "Thanks for the tip," I said, gulping down the coffee.

"Hey, you take care. Stop by the next time you're in."

"Will do. Thanks again."

I spotted Hitchens walking beside Octavia the second I left the bar. He was wearing a vacation shirt of some sort. The same kind they sold in the local gift shop.

"Do you like it?" he asked, grinning.

"He bought it upstairs at the hotel," said Octavia, shaking her head. "I told him not to."

"Nonsense," said Hitchens. "I think it's rather fitting."

"You should listen to your assistant," I said. "Are you two ready?"

They both gave me a nod and we began walking through the promenade, which to my surprise was far less congested than normal. In fact, I was pretty sure I'd never seen it this empty. There were, at most, two dozen people quietly walking between the different shops—a stark contrast to the typical crowds I might normally have to wade through.

I stopped as Ollie's shop came into view on the other end of the promenade. The shutter was closed, something I'd only seen once in the three years I'd known the man.

"Is something wrong, Captain?" asked Hitchens.

"Can you wait here? I need to go and have a look."

"Certainly." He looked at his apprentice. "Octavia, let's have ourselves a seat at that restaurant. Shall we?"

"I could use the meal," she answered.

"Salad for me," he said, rubbing his belly.

"You always say that, but you just end up getting a steak."

He chuckled. "It's a problem." They started to leave. "We'll be over here when you're ready, Captain."

I nodded, then proceeded to Ollie's shop. As I drew closer, I saw there was a sign posted.

CLOSED – STATION SECURITY

The only other time I had seen this Ollie shut down the shop was when he had a run-in with a rogue trash dispenser. The machine malfunctioned as he was trying to dig out some discarded metal, severing three of his fingers in the process. Much to everyone's shock, he had to close the business for nearly twelve hours while he sat in the medbay getting them sewn back on.

When it happened, he didn't bother with a sign. This one said it was from Security, which was even stranger.

"Hey," I heard a voice say from behind me.

I turned to see a girl standing there, chewing on some gum and crossing her arms. It was one of the shoe shop girls from across the divide. I recognized her face because she was always staring at me when I came to Ollie's shop. "Yeah?" I said.

"You lookin' for the guy who runs this place?" She had obnoxiously bright clothes and too much jewelry.

"Sure. You know where he is?" I asked.

She nodded, her long earrings clanging against her neck. "Oh dear, oh dear. You seem like a nice fella. I'm sorry to have to tell you, but he's dead."

For a second, I thought I must have misheard her, she was speaking so fast. "What was that?"

"That guy, the one who owns this place. He's dead, honey. They found him a few hours ago with a bullet in his head. To think, something like that would happen here."

I looked back at the sign. "What the...?" I whispered, totally in disbelief. "Ollie's...dead?"

"Oh, honey, it's such a scandal. The whole floor's talking about it. Me and the other girls are thinking it's probably a hit, you know? Like maybe someone was after him. Danni said she heard from her cousin that Paule over at the bar had something to do with it, but I know Paule and he ain't the kind of guy, you know? He wouldn't go and—"

I blinked, trying to focus on the sign in front of me. Maybe if I went and talked to Security, they could tell me what happened. Hopefully this woman was making everything up, or maybe she was just stupid.

I turned away from both her and the shop. "Thanks. I have to go," I said.

"All right, mister. You take care. Try not to end up like that guy. Be careful."

I didn't answer. "Dammit, Ollie," I muttered as I left that section of the promenade.

Hitchens waved at me as I passed the restaurant. He took a bite from a steak, a large grin on his face. He started to rise from his seat, but I motioned for him to sit, so he did.

"I have to go talk to Security," I said, when I got near their table.

"Is everything okay?" asked Octavia. "You look disturbed."

"Just wait for me here. If I'm not back in a few hours, go to the hotel and join the others. I'll call you."

Despite their clear confusion, they both nodded. "We'll do as you ask," said Octavia.

"Thanks," I said.

Hitchens raised his finger. "Captain, if I might. You look a bit concerned. Are you certain everything is—"

"Just stay out of trouble," I said, then turned and left the restaurant.

What that woman had told me had to be wrong. There was

no way Ollie could be dead. Not that squirrely little jackass. Not in a million years.

It just wasn't possible.

\* \* \*

The Security clerk sat behind the counter with his blue suit and a thin pair of glasses. "Ollie Trinidad? Yes, I do believe he passed away this morning."

I felt my shoulders tense. "The owner of—"

"Taurus Gifts and Memorabilia," finished the clerk. "That's the one. Are you a family member?"

"No. Can you tell me what happened?"

"Only part of it. I'm afraid the investigation is currently still open, which means we can't disclose some of the details. I'm sure you understand."

"Can you at least tell me how he died?"

The clerk looked at his screen for a moment. "It seems he was shot late last night. Could I take down your information? If you're an associate of Mr. Trinidad's, Sergeant Deekon will probably want to ask you some questions."

I turned and walked to the door. "Thanks for your help."

The clerk didn't press me for a name, most likely because their cameras would pull my ID as soon as I left. If they connected the dots and learned about my association with Ollie, I'd have them breathing down my neck before the end of the day.

Several televisions were mounted along the corridor walls, displaying various criminals and missing civilians. I saw a boy who had disappeared a few months ago named Connor Luce, six years old.

### MISSING – CONNOR LUCE
AGE: 6

HAIR COLOR: BLACK

EYE COLOR: HAZEL

IMPORTANT NOTE: PLEASE REPORT SIGHTINGS TO YOUR

LOCAL SECURITY OFFICE.

THANK YOU.

Beside him, I saw the photo of a man with orange hair and freckles. He had a thick pair of glasses and messy clothes.

### WANTED – LANDON O'TOOLE
AGE: 52

HAIR COLOR: RED

EYE COLOR: GREEN

HEIGHT: 6'3"

CRIMES: SIX COUNTS OF MURDER, ARSON, GRAND THEFT

BEWARE: SUSPECT IS ARMED AND CONSIDERED EXTREMELY

DANGEROUS.

The next display, which had been dimly lit until I was close enough for the sensor to pick me up. When it did, the screen brightened, and I saw a familiar face that gave me pause.

On it, there was a woman, dressed in holy garments. My eyes widened as I realized who it was.

**WANTED - ABIGAIL PRYAR**
AGE: 35
HAIR COLOR: BLONDE
EYE COLOR: GREEN
HEIGHT: 5'10''
CRIMES: MURDER, THEFT, ASSAULT, CONSPIRACY TO COMMIT MURDER, KIDNAPPING
BEWARE: SUSPECT IS ARMED AND CONSIDERED EXTREMELY DANGEROUS.

I stared at the image, a little beside myself. I had known she had a warrant out for her arrest, but to see it here on Taurus was surprising. We weren't in Union space, which should have meant any criminal acts performed in Union territory were null and void. That didn't mean the person couldn't be pursued, just that their crimes weren't publicized. Not out here in the Deadlands.

If we started doing that, half the people in this region would be placed under arrest, myself included.

I turned and continued walking, leaving the screen with Abigail's face behind me. I had other things to worry about right now.

As I rounded the corner and entered the promenade, I saw the closed shutters of Ollie's shop and the unusually thin crowd of visitors walking through the deck.

To my surprise, however, there were now three individuals standing together in front of the gate to Ollie's place. Each of them wore a uniform, but it wasn't the kind one might expect to see on Taurus Station.

Blue and gold colors, tight fitting jackets, and pressed collars. Those were Union personnel.

I froze where I stood, staring out across the promenade at the three strangers. What were they doing in front of Ollie's? For that matter, what were they even doing on this station?

I tapped my ear, activating the com to my ship. "Siggy, you picking this up?"

"Naturally, sir," replied the A.I.

"Can you check for any Union ships in the area? See if any are docked."

There was a quick pause. "I'm detecting two ships on the other side of the station. Both are Union, Alpha-class."

I cursed under breath, glancing at the men again. As I stood there, one turned and, for a brief second, we made eye contact.

I doubled back around and walked inside the corridor leading toward Security. This section of the hall was empty, except for a trash dispenser and a small television, which showed a commercial for Jarro's restaurant on a loop.

"Siggy, can you put a call in to Abigail's room at the hotel?"

"Certainly, sir," said Sigmond.

"Hey, you," said a voice from behind me, near the bustling

promenade.

I turned to see one of the Union guys staring at me. The same one who had locked eyes with me before. "Yeah? What do you want?" I asked, casually.

"What's your name?" asked the man.

"Why do you wanna know?"

His two buddies were beside him, each one staring at me. "We're with the Union government and we'd like to ask you a few questions."

"What's the Union doing all the way out here?" I asked.

"That's not your concern. Now, tell us who you are and why you went to Security asking about Mr. Trinidad."

Shit, I thought. I knew I shouldn't have gone there. What was I thinking?

"Come on, sir," said one of the men. "Don't make us arrest you for disrupting an investigation."

"I do odd jobs for Ollie," I said, bending the truth a little. "He owes me money for the last one. I was trying to collect."

"Odd jobs? Like what?"

"I collect trash for him so he can make those ornaments. You saw them in the shop, yeah? That's how he makes them. Just takes wires from dumpsters. Well, I do some collecting for him. Helps pay my rent, you know?"

They all looked at each other. "You collect dumpster wire?"

"Not all the time. Do I look like a two-bit dumpster diver?" I asked. "Sometimes I get other things, too. Just the other day I found a stack of vintage Solento goggles. You know how much those things go for?" I scoffed. "We're talking a few hundred creds, let me tell you."

"What else do you know about the owner of that store?"

"Nothing, except that he buys a lot of wiring and junk. Biggest sucker on the station."

"Wires, huh? Have you ever seen anyone suspicious come into the shop?"

"Like a criminal?" I asked, pretending to be shocked.

"Sure," said the man. "A thief, a brigand, a Renegade-type of character."

"Oh, a Renegade? Now that you mention it, there was this one guy. I saw him with a woman. He came into that shop and then left. That was a week ago. I think his name was Landon."

"Are you certain that was it?" asked the first.

"Something like that. Or Lando. I don't know. He said something about taking off to Arcadia."

"That sounds right," said the second guy. "That's where she's from."

"There's nothing there now," said the third.

"They could have gone further into the Deadlands," said the first.

I faked a sigh. "Look, fellas. I hate to leave you, but I need to get back to work. There's a load of trash I gotta sort through before I can call it a day."

"Wait a second. Tell us about that man you saw. What did he look like?"

I shrugged. "Red hair, I think. Actually, there's a poster of him back there. You see the displays in the hall?"

The man's eyes widened. "Are you talking about Landon O'Toole?"

"Yeah, that's the guy. Pretty scary. I wouldn't want to be stuck in a room with him."

"When did you see him?"

"A few days ago," I said, tapping my chin. "Yeah, maybe in the afternoon sometime."

"Holy shit," said the second guy. "We need to inform Command."

"Easy," insisted the first. "Let's check security footage first."

"Right, right."

"Come on," said the third, pushing past me.

The other two followed, heading to the Security office. When they arrived, they'd spend several hours trying to locate the man on the wanted poster, ultimately coming up empty.

At that point, they'd try their best to track me down. Hell, they might just find the security footage of me arriving with Abigail and Lex.

Not that it would matter. By the time they discovered the truth, I'd be halfway through a slip tunnel, gone to some undisclosed location.

I just had to move my ass before it was too late.

# SEVENTEEN

I disappeared into the elevator at the end of the promenade, hitting the button for deck 12, where the hotel waited.

While the doors closed, I tapped my ear and opened the com. "Any word from Abigail, Siggy?"

"I was about to tell you, sir. I have her on the line."

"Patch her in."

"Hello?" asked Abigail.

"Hey, it's Jace. I need you to listen up."

"Oh, is everything all right, Captain?"

"How fast can you get your shit and meet me in the hotel lobby?"

"What? Why are you asking?"

"The Union is here," I explained. "They're looking for both of us."

There was a short break of silence. "I understand. Everyone's here in the room. We can be ready in ten minutes."

"Leave whatever you don't need. Tell the others to hurry, otherwise we're all fucked."

"Is that Mr. Hughes?" I heard Lex ask. "Tell him I said, hi!"

"Just a second, sweety," Abigail said in a soft voice. "Captain, are you absolutely certain about what you saw?"

The doors opened and two men, each dressed in a Union uniform, stood in front of me.

I swallowed hard.

Each of them looked at me. "Excuse us," said the first one, a tall, pale fellow with white hair.

"Captain, did you hear me?" Abigail asked. "I asked if you're sure."

"I'm sure," I said, then clicked off the com.

The two men looked at me, lifting their brows. "Pardon?" asked the second guy, who was thicker than his friend, with brown hair.

The door closed and the two men just stood there.

I glanced up at the display, which read deck 9. Still a few more left to go before the hotel. "Which floor?" I asked, hovering my finger over the screen.

The first one nodded. "Twelve. Thanks."

I pulled my finger back from the display.

*Well, shit.*

* * *

The two Union officers and I stepped out of the elevator and onto the hotel floor. I debated turning back around, but stopped myself, since it would look suspicious.

Better to wait here, as I planned. If these two jackasses didn't leave by the time Abigail was here, I'd call and tell her to standby.

I felt the weight of my pistol resting beneath my coat. *Not yet*, I told myself.

The two men walked to the front desk and started talking to the receptionist.

I sat on a bench, far enough so I couldn't hear them, although that also meant they wouldn't hear me. I tapped my ear and opened a channel. "Siggy, put Abigail through," I whispered, turning my head away from the men.

A second later, I heard the nun's voice. "Captain? What's going on?"

"Don't come out," I muttered. "There's Union officers here. Wait inside until I tell you, and be ready."

"Okay…just a moment," she said, and I heard shuffling sounds on the other side of the line. "This way, Lex. Stay here, right behind me. Yes, right there. Good girl. Okay, Captain, we're standing by for your mark."

"Excuse me, sir," I heard a voice say.

I turned my head back to see the white-haired officer looking down at me. "Uh, yeah?"

His partner was still at the desk, talking to the clerk.

"Why are you sitting here alone? Are you waiting for someone?" asked the white-haired man.

"I wanted to rest my feet," I said.

"Why not return to your room?" he asked.

I clenched my teeth. What was this guy's problem? A sudden urge to grab my pistol rose in my stomach, but I suppressed it. "I'm fine here."

He gave me a look that told me my statement wasn't enough. I'd have to embellish something.

With a dramatic sigh, I crossed my arms. "If you must know, pal, I have a bladder problem and pissed the bed last night. It's a serious medical problem and I'm not proud of it."

"You...did what?" the guy asked, looking down at my crotch.

"Oh yeah, like you didn't hear me. Look, I was just on Praxus III and I slept with the wrong girl. Is that what you wanna hear? Damn bladder's out of control."

He took a step back. "Oh, that's disgusting."

"Yeah, thanks for making me relive it." I got to my feet. "I can't wait to get my ass home. No more vacations for me."

"Sorry to bother you," said the officer. He went back to the counter to join his friend, a disturbed look in his eyes.

*Asshole*, I thought.

The two men took a card from the clerk before turning to leave. "Let's start with room 201 and go from there," said the white-haired man.

They passed me and began heading through the hall to my left. There were only two directions and I had no idea which one had Abigail's room.

I tapped my ear again. "Abigail? You read me?"

The line clicked. "One moment, sir," said Siggy. "Connecting you."

"Hello?" said the nun.

"What room are you in?" I asked her, quickly.

"212," she said. "Why?"

I glanced at the sign on the wall near the elevator. Odd numbers to the left, even numbers to the right.

I leaned to the side and glanced at the two Union officers. "Wait for my signal," I told Abigail. "Just a second."

"Right," she answered. "Everyone, stay close and be ready."

I watched the two men touch the door with the card the clerk had given them. A moment later, it opened, and they began talking to the person inside. I couldn't hear the conversation, but they seemed to have little trouble getting the resident to let them in.

As they disappeared into the room, I got to my feet. "Now, come out and move!"

I heard a door open on the other side of the hall. A crowd of familiar faces unloaded from the room, carrying luggage and hurrying toward me. Abigail, Lex, Freddie, Hitchens, and Octavia were all here and ready to go.

I hit the elevator button, not realizing that it would take a few seconds for the lift to reach us. Why hadn't I thought of bringing it up sooner?

Abigail came up to my side in a mad hurry. "What's the problem?"

"Elevator. Just hang on."

"Mr. Hughes? What are you doing here?" asked Lex.

"He's here to help," said Freddie. "Right, Captain?"

The elevator arrived and the doors opened. "Get inside," I told them.

I heard the sound of another door opening, the one the two officers had gone into. They entered the hall, glancing at me and the rest of the group.

The older man seemed to notice my fellow passengers. Specifically, the little albino girl with white hair standing beside me. "Hey! You, there!"

As the doors closed in front of me, I waved at the two men. *Bye-bye*, I mouthed.

We descended from the upper deck and toward the bottom promenade. No doubt, the two idiot officers would inform their superiors within seconds. It wouldn't be long before I had a swarm of soldiers coming after me.

That was only if I couldn't reach my ship, of course. *The Renegade Star* was docked pretty close, but we'd have to move quickly.

"Let's go!" I snapped as soon as the doors opened.

"Were those men with the Union?" asked Freddie as we

began to move.

"What do you think?" I asked, rather bluntly. I went straight into the sea of civilians on the promenade, pushing them aside to make space for the others as they struggled to keep up.

We entered the main section of the shopping plaza, sluggishly wading through the mob. Hitchens was the slowest, stumbling to keep up, and scared shitless. He didn't belong here, dodging Union officers and running for his freedom. None of these people did.

Behind us, an alarm sounded, and then it was everywhere at once. Two dozen red lights swirling on the walls. Holo-displays emitted warning signs, letting people know to take cover.

That was when I heard the gunshot. It was so loud that I couldn't tell the direction.

A woman screamed, not far from where we were. The mob panicked, stumbling over each other, tripping and screaming as the frenzy and fear set in throughout the station.

The already thin crowd in the promenade dispersed, running into the nearby shops, which were closing their shutters in anticipation of what was about to unfold.

Another shot, and then I heard a man yell, "Stop them!"

I looked and saw three security personnel standing beside two Union soldiers. Only the soldiers had weapons, and they drew them in a hurry.

In a swift and fluid motion, I turned and unholstered my

pistol, aiming with my body as I brought the men into my sights.

I pulled the trigger, the first shot striking the soldier directly in the side of his belly, pushing him back against the wall.

The second officer took aim at me, but before he could shoot, I sent a second round his way, striking his leg. He screamed, violently, and blindly fired the rifle in our direction.

Bullets soared through the promenade, hitting the walls behind me. One of the displays to my right shattered, scattering glass onto the floor.

"Move!" I yelled, grabbing Hitchens by the shoulder and shoving him. "Get your asses to *The Star*!"

Freddie was on his knees, clutching his arm, blood dripping between his fingers. I went to him and hoisted his arm over my shoulder. "Freddie! Get your ass up!"

"S-Sorry," he muttered, a confused look in his eyes. "I'm sorry, Jace."

Abigail came running, taking Freddie from me. "I've got him! We need you to cover us!"

I let him go and turned my attention back to the guards. The remaining security officers were making their way through the promenade, ready to put us on the floor. I raised my gun and fired above them, shattering one of the overhead lights. It sent sparks raining down on them, making them panic. "Back off or I'll lay you out right here!" I shouted as I aimed the pistol at them.

They froze, raising their hands. They didn't get paid enough to press this, unlike the Union soldiers who were currently writhing in pain behind them.

Abigail and Freddie continued on ahead of me, followed by Hitchens and Octavia. I waited for them to reach the docking bay at the end of the promenade, close to where my ship was waiting. We were almost there. I just had to hold this line for a little while longer.

The same elevators we'd used before suddenly dinged, and the doors slid open. The two men from the hotel appeared inside, making eye contact with me immediately. The one with the white hair dropped his mouth and pointed to me, while the other went for his gun.

Good thing I was faster.

I fired at them, hitting one in the shoulder. The two men ducked back inside, and unloading my entire magazine, buckling the elevator doors as they closed.

Without a second beat, I reloaded, darting my eyes between the elevator and the other set of guards across the promenade.

A loud cry jarred me, pulling my attention. It sounded like a small child. I scanned my eyes across the warzone, trying to find the one responsible.

"Make it stop!" screamed Lex. I turned to see her crouching several meters behind me, ducked beneath a large bench. How did she end up here alone? Why wasn't she with the others?

I ran over to her, taking her by the wrist. "Get your ass to the ship, kid!"

Then there was a gunshot, and a bullet buzzed by me, hitting the wall behind us. The injured soldier that I'd downed was on his ass, struggling with his rifle. Before he could pull the trigger, I reacted without thinking, twisting where I stood and firing a single shot at him. The bullet struck his throat, shattering half his neck like a pimple, and he grasped desperately at his missing flesh. I was about to do the same to the other men beside him when I felt Lex tugging at my arm. "Mr. Hughes!"

I blinked, stopping myself. I had to get this kid to the ship. I had to get off this station. If I didn't get her out of here now, she might end up dead.

I took the girl in my arms. "Hold onto me!"

She put her arms around my neck, squeezing me with more strength than I thought she had in her, and I darted towards the dock where my ship was waiting.

One of the two men from the elevator screamed in the distance, calling for more men, but we were already gone, running down the corridor.

Abigail and Octavia were waiting at the airlock for us, panic on their faces. "Oh gods!" shouted Abby, letting out her arms to take the girl.

I handed off the kid, then motioned for everyone to get inside the airlock. "Next time, keep a better eye on your shit, lady!"

I slammed my first on the release button, closing the doors. "Everyone alive?" I asked, holstering my gun. "Okay, good. Siggy, get us the hell out of here. Everyone else, strap yourselves in!"

# EIGHTEEN

"I'm afraid Taurus Station isn't allowing us to separate," said Sigmond.

"Attention vessel attempting to flee," said a voice over the com. "Set down your weapons and prepare to be boarded."

"As I was saying," remarked the A.I.

"Can you override the controls?" I asked.

"Station Security has initiated lockdown procedures, making it impossible."

I looked at my passengers. "Anyone know how to hack a security system?"

None of them answered.

"That's what I was afraid of," I said, looking back to the airlock.

"Captain, I could attempt to pull us free, although the damage to the station would be significant," said Sigmond.

"How bad?"

"The force of our pull would break the docking clamp from the wall and it would leave a sizeable hole behind."

"Would anyone be injured?"

"Not if they follow procedure," theorized Sigmond. "The station walls should compensate by raising a shield to conceal the damage and protect station personnel from exposure."

"What about damage to the ship?"

"Our hull would take some moderate strain, though it would remain intact. Atmosphere would be unaffected."

"Captain, are you actually considering forcing our way free from the station?" asked Hitchens.

"The alternative is worse, trust me," I said.

He dabbed his forehead with his red handkerchief. "Oh, goodness."

"Let's do it, Siggy. Yank us free, and as soon as we're away from the station, I want you to open a tunnel."

"What coordinates, sir?"

"Doesn't matter," I said. "The opposite of Union space. I don't give a shit."

"That would be further into the Deadlands, towards Sarkonian occupied space," said Siggy.

The thought of taking my ship anywhere near Sarkonian territory made me sick, but it was better than risking the Union finding us. "That'll work, just cloak us when we get there. We're laying low for a while."

"Right away, sir. All passengers, please fasten your safety harness and remain calm."

Abigail looked at me as she clutched Lex in her arms. "Are you sure about this?"

I gave her a nod. "Trust me."

I felt a vibration beneath my feet, a humming sound all through the ship, and it lingered for a moment as we all looked at each other. The thrusters were powering on, already beginning to burn.

Things were about to get bumpy.

I looked at the others. "Everyone hold onto some—"

The entire ship jerked, sending me to my knees as I gripped the railing along the wall. I held on tight with both my hands. Grinding sounds were coming from outside the ship, near the airlock.

I glanced at my passengers. Abigail and Lex had strapped themselves in, along with Freddie, who was still bleeding from his fresh wound. Octavia had her arms around Hitchens, who had also fallen to the floor. I heard a loud blast from beyond the airlock, followed by a series of rapid clicks.

Then, a sudden jerk forward.

The shaking stopped immediately, and I was able to get back on my feet. "Everyone okay?" I asked, looking first at Lex.

"We're okay," said Abigail.

"Us, too," said Hitchens.

I went to the window to see the damage. The docking platform was torn to pieces, with chunks of debris floating outside the gaping, monstrous hole in the station's wall.

A layer of metal slid down over it, shielding the deck from within, protecting the station from exposure.

As we made our escape, I noticed something trailing behind us—a large chunk of the wall, stuck to our airlock.

I'd have to deal with that later.

"Siggy, let's go!" I barked.

"Opening a Tunnel," said the A.I.

"Where are we going?" asked Lex.

I started moving to the front of the ship. "As far as we can get," I said as I left the lounge.

Inside the cockpit, the interface was already live and waiting for my authorization. The second I was seated, I tapped the activation button, launching a beam and opening a tunnel directly ahead.

As we entered it, I activated the ship's rear camera, focusing on the station. There was no going back now. I was pretty certain this was the last time I'd ever get to lay my eyes on it, the closest thing I had to a home.

An image of Ollie swept through my mind, right as the tunnel closed behind us. *I'm sorry, Ollie,* I thought as I watched the station disappear. *I'm so fucking sorry.*

* * *

"So much for that," said Octavia as I walked back into the lounge. She was sitting beside Freddie, tending to his wound with my first-aid kit. They didn't seem to notice me yet.

Freddie let out a cough. "What are we going to do now? The Union is after us. The church is gone. We're running out of options."

"We're staying the course," said Abigail.

"Which is what, exactly?" I interrupted, walking further into the room.

She looked at me. "The rediscovery of Earth, obviously."

"That again?" I asked.

"I know you don't believe us, Captain, and that's okay," she said. "All I ask is that you take us somewhere safe for the time being. A neutral planet, if possible, far from Union-controlled space. Somewhere where we can charter another ship."

"I'll drop you at Keasler Station. It's near a mining colony. Not much around it, but far enough that you won't have to worry about being caught. They also have a decent spaceport there, so I'm sure you can find someone to take you where you wanna go."

"We appreciate it," said Abigail.

"Mr. Hughes isn't coming?" asked Lex, looking up at her.

"I've got other things I have to do. Sorry kid."

Namely, paying Fratley the money I owed, and I'd have to do it soon. The deadline was fast approaching and the last thing I needed was more of *this* to deal with.

I went to my bunk and collapsed into the mattress, but didn't sleep. I couldn't, not with Ollie's face still in my head. The poor bastard's death was all my fault.

What was I doing, shuttling these fugitives around the Deadlands? Was the money worth the price of my friend's life?

What was I thinking?

\* \* \*

I slept for ten hours.

When I finally woke up, the clock said it was the early morning. Had I gone to bed at a normal time, I'd probably still be asleep.

I found Freddie in the lounge, asleep with a patch on his shoulder. He seemed to be doing all right, breathing soundly and staying quiet. Beside him, Octavia was resting with a pad in her hand, lightly snoring.

I left them there and continued into the cockpit. I sat down in my chair and stared out into the swirling green walls of the slip tunnel. It was both beautifully chaotic and frightening, all at the same time. I could've watched it for hours, just like I'd done so many times before. In all the universe, as far as I'd found, there was nothing as mysterious or divine as the glow of slipspace. If I'd been a religious man, like the passengers I was carrying on my boat, I might've found something holy in all of this. Something to inspire me.

To move me.

But those things had always been for others, I knew. *Like*

*Freddie and Abby,* I thought. *Better people than me.*

I hated myself for being the skeptic, for being unable to see the magic, but wasn't it worse to lie to yourself? To deny what you were and what you believed?

No matter how much I might have tried, I could never see what the rest of them did. Never see the gods in the stars.

*I could only be me.*

"Sir," said Sigmond. The word brought me out of my head.

"What is it?" I asked.

"We are currently nearing the end of the ninth slip tunnel since we departed Taurus Station," said the A.I.

"Nine, already?" I asked, pulling up the galactic map. It looked like we'd gone in a crazy zigzag after leaving the station. Standard protocol when evading an enemy like the Union.

By the look of it, we appeared to be fairly close to Keasler. It wouldn't take us long to reach it, and then I'd drop the others off and be on my way.

On my way? To where, I wondered.

First to Fratley, I supposed, but then I wasn't sure. I couldn't go back to Taurus, especially with the Union after me. Maybe I'd head to Ouros and lay low for a while, bury my head in the sand of some beach and forget my shit-storm of a life. "What's our ETA to Keasler?" I asked.

"Three standard hours, sir."

"Not long," I said, and suddenly it felt very cold.

"Shall I wake the passengers and inform them?" asked Sigmond.

I leaned back in my chair and watched the waves and sparks along the walls of the tunnel. "No," I said, taking a long sigh. "Let them sleep a while longer."

\* \* \*

We left the final tunnel and entered the outer rim of the Keasler system. Several ships appeared on the grid, most of which were docked at the station, but I noticed several others departing and arriving from the mining colony on the fourth planet from the star.

I'd only been here once before, a few years back when I was on a delivery mission. A guy named Oxam Wu asked me to drop some illegal goods off on the station for the administrator at the time. I was less experienced, so I asked fewer questions. It wasn't until later that I realized I was actually carrying weapons. Not my finest hour, but I always made sure to understand my jobs better after that.

Maybe that was a mistake, though. Asking questions is how I got into this mess in the first place. If I'd never pressed Abigail about what she was carrying, I could've avoided the Union altogether. Ollie and Bron would be alive.

I shook my head. It was too late to think about alternatives. This was my life now. Better to deal with shit than look back.

I kept my distance from the station. "Let's wait until we're ready," I told Siggy.

"Shall I cloak the ship, sir?"

"Park us behind this moon for now," I said, tapping the display.

"Sir, Ms. Pryar would like to see you," said Sigmond.

"Guess that means she's awake," I said.

Freddie and Octavia were both still in the lounge, although the priest was still passed out. Octavia was in the middle of replacing his bandage when I came out of the cockpit. "Good morning, Captain," she said when she saw me.

"How's he doing?" I asked.

"Holding together. He had a slight fever during the night, but it appears to have broken."

"Glad to hear it. Let me know if you need anything."

She nodded. "Thank you."

Abigail's room was down the hall opposite mine. Her door was already open. I noticed a bag on the bed, open with clothes in it. "Getting ready to go?" I asked, stepping inside.

Lex was in the corner, watching the nun fill her luggage. "She's in a hurry," said the girl.

"That so?" I asked.

"We have to get going as soon as we're docked," said Abigail. "Sigmond told me we're in the system, so it's almost time."

"I don't want to leave again," said Lex. "This ship is nice."

"Kid's got good taste," I said.

"Nevertheless, since you can't be bothered to help us any further—"

"You know I have to take care of my own shit, Abby. It's not about you."

She tossed a shirt into her bag. "Okay."

"If I brought you with me to Fratley, he'd kill me and take Lex, all so he could get that bounty. It would be a disaster."

"I know."

"Then, why are you upset?"

"I'm not upset," she said. "I just think it would be easier for everyone if we didn't have to find another ship."

"What did you call me in here for? To yell at me?"

She sighed. "No, I'm sorry. That's not—"

"Then what is it?"

She stopped, hesitating for a moment, then touched her pocket. "I wanted to give you something before you left."

"You got me a present?" I asked.

"No, don't be ridiculous. It's something I owe you. That's all."

"Oh. Like money?"

She reached into her pocket and took out what appeared to be a gold locket. "Here," she said, dropping it in my hand.

The small chain dangled off my finger. "What is this?"

"It's your payment," she said, turning back to her clothes.

"My payment?"

Upon closer inspection, I saw an intricately carved pattern of a planet on the top. It was the same one, I realized, that Freddie had shown me several days ago on his pad. "Is this supposed to be Earth?"

"That's what they say," she replied. "You can sell it if you want. Go ahead and open it."

I pulled the two sides apart, only to find a ticking clock inside. This thing wasn't a locket; it was a pocket-watch. "Holy shit."

"It's solid gold," she said. "The church believed it was a relic from Earth. I don't know for certain, but now it's yours. It should cover what I owe you for helping Lex and me."

"I already have all the money I need from those machines we sold. You paid me, fair and square."

"That was for the second job you did, taking us to Epsilon. This watch is for helping me. Take it, Mr. Hughes. Please."

I looked at the gold trinket in my hand. It was pristine and glistening. "You're sure?"

"I am," she responded, stuffing her luggage tight with clothes. "Thank you again for everything you've done."

* * *

Returning to the cockpit, I felt the pocket-watch clinging noisily in my jacket. It was heavy in a good way, and it felt natural on my person. It was a fine gift, and despite the high price it might fetch on the market, I wouldn't sell it. I had all the money I needed to pay Fratley back, plus a bit extra.

As I neared the end of the hall, I heard the com system click on. "Sir, may I have your attention?" asked Sigmond.

"What is it?" I asked.

"The slip tunnel we left on our arrival is opening. Shall we remain at our present location or would you prefer we move?"

"It better not be the Union again." I watched the display as a ship came flying out of the tunnel, recognizing it instantly.

"I don't believe it is," said Sigmond.

It was the same ship I'd seen above Arcadia, the one belonging to Fratley. "Siggy, get ready to do another slip!"

"Sir, a channel is opening. It's—"

"Well, ain't this a surprise?" asked a familiar voice.

"Fratley?"

"That's right, buddy. Good to see you again. Mind if I ask what you're doing all the way out here?"

I touched the control panel, trying to bring up the com systems. Nothing happened. "Siggy, you there?"

"I took control of the com," said Fratley. "Hope that's all right. I wanted your full attention."

"You hacked my ship?"

"Hacked might not be the right word," he said. "I have the backdoor access codes. It's just good business, you know? Makes it easier to repossess my property if the payment doesn't come through."

"Fratley, I was just about to come see you, once this job was done. I've got your money sitting in my account right now."

"Oh? All one seventy-five thousand creds?"

"Plus some interest," I said.

He laughed. "Ain't that something? I guess that goes to show what a little motivation can do! You put some fire under someone's ass and they'll always get the job done."

"If you want, I'll transfer the credits to your account right now. I just need a gal-net uplink. I can't do that without my com, though."

"Fair enough, Jace. I'll let you pay me, but that'll have to wait. The people you're transporting, I need 'em."

A nervous chill ran down my arm. Had I heard him correctly? No, there was no way he knew who I had on my ship. He couldn't. "Excuse me?"

"Don't play stupid. I know you've got that Pryar woman with you. Probably got the albino freak, too. You hand them over, then pay me what you owe. We'll call it square after that."

*Shit*, I thought.

"Don't try to run, either," warned Fratley. "I've got three quads locked on your position. We'll blast you right out of that moon's orbit."

I knew Fratley could see through my cloak, so he wasn't bluffing. I could try running, but faster ships than mine had tried and now they were space dust. Besides, I'd watched him follow others for as long as it took, just to see them dead. He'd probably do the same to me. "Okay, Fratley. I'll stay put."

"Good man, Jace. That's what I like to hear!"

The com clicked off. "Sir, I apologize," said Sigmond. "I lost control of the system."

"Is the ship okay?" I asked.

"Nothing has been damaged."

"Activate your firewall. Don't let him take over again."

"Yes, sir."

I leapt out of my seat and ran into the lounge. "Everyone, get out here!"

Octavia, Freddie, and Hitchens were already there, but Abigail and Lex came running. "What is it?" asked the nun.

"Fratley's back," I said, pointing out the window. "And he knows you're with me."

# NINETEEN

"What are we going to do?" asked Hitchens.

"We have to get out of here," insisted Abigail.

"Calm down. I'll figure something out," I said.

"Sir, the ravager ship is deploying a shuttle. They wish for us to let them dock," informed Sigmond.

"Put me through to Fratley," I ordered. "All of you, stay quiet."

Lex was standing between Octavia's arms, watching me. I wondered if she even knew what was going on.

Fratley's voice came over the com. "Jace, what do you want? I'm about to head over there to pick you up."

"There's a problem with my airlock," I said. "It has a wall on it."

"Don't I know it! Relax, Jace. I've got you covered. My boys will rip that shit right off so fast you'll forget it was even there. Just get ready, because they might accidentally penetrate your ship's atmosphere and kill everyone inside." He let out a long chuckle.

"If I die, you won't get your money," I cautioned.

"You let me worry about that," said Fratley. "All right. Stand by!"

The line clicked and he was gone. I peered out the window to see the shuttle inbound from his ship.

"We need to hide you," I said to everyone on my ship. "All of you."

"Are we going back in the hole?" asked Lex. "I don't like it down there. It smells like pee."

"It'll be over soon," said Abigail, stroking the girl's hair.

"You all remember where to go, right? Sigmond will open the wall when you're ready," I said.

"We'll head there now," said Octavia, taking Hitchens by the hand.

"Oh, goodness," said Hitchens.

I looked at Freddie, who was holding his shoulder. "You think you can go with them?" I asked him.

Freddie got to his feet. "Don't worry about me. I'll be okay."

I nodded. "Octavia, look after him. Take the med kit."

Fratley's shuttle was arriving outside, quickly releasing two extendable arms. They gripped the massive block of metal that was still attached to my airlock. For a second, I thought it might end with a breach in my ship, but I was relieved to see that this wasn't the case. Instead, the wreckage detached, and Fratley's shuttle released it into empty space, letting it float away.

I turned to look at Octavia. "Quick, I'll help you to your spot. There's not much time, so we'll have to hurry."

* * *

The airlock opened, and Fratley Oxanos walked into my ship. "Jace!" he exclaimed. "You old rat."

"Fratley," I said, no enthusiasm in my voice.

He beamed a wicked smile. "Thanks for having me."

Eight of his men unloaded behind him, each of them carrying a rifle and a sidearm.

Fratley looked at the nearest one, the squad leader. "Start the search."

"Yes, Boss," replied the man. He motioned for the others to follow, and together they ran by me and into the lounge.

Fratley and I both looked at each other. "It feels like I was just here," he said.

"I guess you must really like the coffee," I answered.

He laughed. "You know, back when I was a Renegade, I had a ship just like yours. It was nicer, of course, but still pretty similar."

"Is that right?"

He nodded. "I'm telling you, I was on top of my game back then. Jobs were easy to get, you know. Not like today. I had enough cash to pay my debts and fix my ship, which is more than I can say for you."

"It's been a slow season. We have the Union to thank for that."

"Right, that's true. The Union's been down everyone's neck to play nice and do as we're told. They're inside the Deadlands now, too, expanding the border. You saw a few on Taurus, except that ain't all of 'em. They've got big plans, Jace."

I was surprised he knew about Taurus. I never saw his ship in the area. "You heard about that, did you?"

"You're a naughty one, Jace. You know, they don't even know it was you, but I was watching."

"Watching?" I repeated.

"Always, when it comes to you, Jace."

I leaned against the wall. "I'm not sure if I should be flattered or concerned."

"It's for your own good. You owe me a small fortune, so I can't let you go and get yourself killed. Not until I get paid, anyway."

"I get it," I said, crossing my arms. "You have a business to look after."

"A very successful one," he corrected.

The head grunt came jogging down the corridor. "Sir, there's no sign of anyone else on the ship."

"Oh?" asked Fratley. He raised his brow at me. "Where's the girl, Jace? You got her stowed away somewhere?"

"Not sure what you mean," I said, looking him right in the eye.

He snickered. "Now, Jace. We both know you've got her hidden somewhere. I saw the security footage from Taurus. She boarded this ship."

"I don't remember that. Must have been a different ship."

He looked at the nearby thug. "One of the crates was moved

out the last time we were here, wasn't it? Let's have a look at the cargo hold."

"Aye, sir."

Fratley made sure I followed him. His thugs pushed me along until we were inside the bay.

The crates were all nestled tight against the wall, having been moved to their original spots. Fratley walked to the nearest one, the same crate that had been pulled out, and examined it. "Let's get this moved, shall we?"

Two broad-chested individuals grabbed the side of the box and pulled it back, sliding it against the metal floor, filling the bay with a loud screech. When they had it cleared, Fratley went to the back wall and leaned in close to look at it.

"Looking for something?" I asked.

He tapped his cane on the wall, and there was a deep thud. "Got yourself a hidden compartment, do you?" He waved one of his men over to him. The lackey handed a small device to him, which Fratley took. "Can't say I blame you. I had a few of my own, back when I was in your shoes."

He pressed a small button on the device, then scanned the wall. Not two seconds later, the compartment raised, revealing itself.

Fratley stared into the empty section of my cargo bay, leaning in, and finding nothing. No signs of any intruders. Not a single trace of any fugitive passengers.

"Satisfied?" I asked.

He peered back at me and smiled. "Not quite yet, I'm afraid."

Fratley tapped the side of his ear, opening a com channel. "Find them yet?" he asked. "Uh huh. Oh, well, that was fast work. Good work."

The ravager boss twirled his cane in the air and began walking back toward me.

"Something going on?" I asked.

"Why don't you follow me, Jace? You'll want to see this."

We left the bay and proceeded down the hall. I could already hear something up ahead, coming from the lounge. There was movement, the sound of someone shuffling their feet, followed by a grunt. "Sit down and don't move," a man snapped.

As we rounded the corner, I already knew what to expect. Abigail came into view right away, her long, brown hair flowing down the side of her neck, followed by a stern look as she stared with those fierce hazel eyes at the three goons standing before her.

Then, as I finally stepped into the lounge, I saw one of the men holding Lex, gripping her shoulder with one hand as well as her white hair with the other.

Fratley smacked his knee. "Hooey! What a sight. Looks like I'm about to get paid! Thanks for keeping these two safe for me, Jace."

Lex's neck was strained, with the man holding her hair so

tight. I could see she was in pain.

Abigail noticed it too, and she set her eyes on the guard's face. I knew the first chance she got, she'd try to kill him. I only hoped she could contain herself long enough for me to figure something out.

"Of all the guys to give me shit, I'm glad I kept you alive, Jace," said Fratley. "I'm about to get paid twice in a single day."

I felt the urge to grab my pistol and shoot this asshole on the spot, but quickly buried the impulse. "How nice for you."

Fratley ignored me, walking to Lex's side. He took her by the jaw and examined her face. "All that money, just for you."

I noticed Abigail tense up, leaning forward a little more, watching the man with the cane.

"I wonder why the Union wants you back so bad," said Fratley. "You got something they need?"

"She's just a kid," I said.

"Weird-looking one, though, ain't she?" he asked, running a finger through her alabaster hair. "Freaky."

"Get your hands off of her!" yelled Abigail, unable to hold back anymore.

Fratley let go and turned to the nun. He took a step closer to her, then raised his cane and struck her, right in the jaw. She fell on the floor, suddenly bleeding and moaning. "What was that?" he asked, calmly standing over her.

"Hey!" I shouted.

Fratley laughed. "Toss me a rag, would you?" he asked one of his men.

I swallowed hard, suddenly afraid that this psychopath would murder someone. "Please, Fratley, just calm down!"

He smiled as he wiped the blood from his cane. "Calm?" he asked, looking at Abigail as she lay on the floor. He kicked her, a sly grin on his face.

Abigail yelped, reaching out with her hand, trying to crawl away.

"Everyone's calm," said Fratley.

"Why don't I get that money over to you, huh? I owe you, what, seventy-five thousand? I'll toss in an extra fifteen. What do you say? Ninety thousand credits, all yours."

Fratley bent back to look at me, arching his eye. He stood there a second, like he was processing what I'd said. Then, he smiled. "Oh, Jace, you know just how to warm my heart." He smacked his cane against heel of his boot. "Let's see those creds!"

"Sigmond, transfer ninety thousand credits to the following account number," I said, looking at Fratley. "Go ahead."

He grinned. "44-029-11000."

"Request acknowledged," said Sigmond. A few seconds passed. "Transfer complete."

Fratley reached out his hand toward the nearest thug. "Pad."

The man retrieved it from his side. "Yes, Boss."

"Let's see," Fratley said, taking the device and examining it.

"Yes. Yes. Here we go."

I said nothing, letting him take as much time as he needed.

"Ah, great job, Jace. It looks like it's all here. Isn't that something?"

"You're welcome," I said.

"Now, we just need to get the little brat over to that Brigham bastard."

"Brigham?"

He fanned his hand dismissively at me. "Forget it. Doesn't matter. All you need to know is that I'm leaving with the kid. There's a warrant for the nun, so I'll be taking her, too." He nodded to the thug hold Lex's shoulder. "Get her on the shuttle and strap her in nice and tight. Same with that one." He pointed to Abigail. "Give her a rag so she stops bleeding everywhere."

The guard forced Lex to stand and nudged her along, toward the back of the lounge. Another two men picked Abigail up, one on each side.

"Are you selling them to the Union?" I asked.

"They want the girl unharmed, but the nun...well, she ain't gotta be in one piece. Might let the boys have some fun before we head back."

I felt my hand squeeze and my chest stiffen.

"As for what to do with you, Jace, I'm a bit torn. Most times, I'd kill a man where he stood for trying to fuck with my bounties, but you did all right getting me that money. I know you're soft on those two, so I'm trying to be reasonable. It's easy for a man to fall for a girl when he's surrounded by the Void. I get that. Hell, I used to do the same shit, back when I was in your shoes. So, I'm thinking it ain't *all* your fault. It's just your dick. You can't help it, right?"

I kept my eyes on Abigail as they carried her away. "Sure," I said, trying to bottle my emotion.

"I'll tell what I'll do, Jace, since I *understand* you so well. I'll let you work it off. You bring me a cut of all your earnings for the next year and maybe I'll forget this ever happened. That'll keep you square with me." He tapped his cane on the floor. "No one else gets a deal like this, buddy. You're *lucky* I like you."

I wanted to reach across the room and bury my pistol in his mouth. This asshole. "Wow, Fratley. I don't know what to say."

"Ain't it the truth? And if you're lucky, maybe I'll extend the deal a bit longer. Just do right by me from now on, because trust me, you don't want to piss me off again. Not after this. You understand? Come on, Jace. I gotta hear you say it. I gotta hear you say you understand."

"I get it, Fratley," I said.

"Good," he responded. "That's *real* good."

"There's a problem with that plan, though, unfortunately," I said, eying the guards as they shoved Lex toward the airlock.

"Oh?" chuckled Fratley. "How's that, Jace? You got a better idea? You want a bigger cut? I'm afraid this is as good as it gets, pal."

"No, that's not it," I said, looking back at him. "I'm not after more cash."

"Then, what?" he asked. "You want me to give you an hour with the nun?"

I stared at him, unblinking, a bead of sweat running down my temple. There was a strong possibility I could die today, and it'd be all my fault for what came next. I could walk away right now and live, take other jobs and do other things, maybe even retire to a resort planet somewhere far away. My life could be a cakewalk, no question about it.

But easy wasn't meant for men like me. No, I liked to play the hard game. I liked to bet it all.

*Fuck it*, I thought, sweeping my hand inside my jacket and clutching the extendable pistol under my belt. "I'll need a bit longer than an hour," I said, tapping a button on the gun, causing it to fully form in my hand. In a solid, quick motion, I brought the barrel out and aimed it straight at Fratley's face. "That is, if you don't mind."

Fratley smirked. "Now what are you gonna do with that little thing, Jace? Kill a bug? You forget I have six guys standing behind you?"

I heard a rifle load. "Put the weapon down!" shouted one of the ravager soldiers.

"Not happening," I said, maintaining my aim. "Try anything

and I'll shoot."

Fratley shook his head. "That'd be a big mistake. Like I said, you pull that trigger and Jimmy over there will blow a hole clean through your skull."

"I guess we'll find out," I said. "Isn't that right, Octavia?"

Fratley raised his eye. "Who the fuck is Oct—"

A bullet exploded from a metal grate above one of the men, striking him in the head and killing him dead. The grate fell from the ceiling, landing on the now deceased guard.

Octavia popped out of the opening above, holding my pistol, and fired two shots at the other nearby men.

A bullet struck the first in the stomach. He staggered, firing his weapon into the ceiling in a panic.

The second shot hit his friend in the foot, ripping the boot to pieces, along with the man's toes, leaving a massive hole where his flesh should be. The man screamed, trying to lift his weapon towards the vent, but before he could, a third bullet hit him in the chest, sending him into the food counter and down to the floor where he lay still.

Octavia Brie dropped from the gap in the ceiling and landed on the body beneath her.

Fratley's eyes widened at the chaos unfolding before him. "Stop her!"

Another soldier took aim, but Octavia struck first. Her shots hit the both the man and the coffee maker behind him, sending shards of glass and black liquid into the air.

Fratley and I both dove to get out of the way, attempting to avoid the storm. We met on the floor, inches from each other's face.

It took us both a second to realize what was happening. I tried to aim the pistol at him, except he reached for my wrist before I could move it. I raised my hand to get some leverage, only to have Fratley slam it back down as he tried to knock the gun away. When I refused to let go, he released the magazine and ejected the loaded round from the chamber, then threw both the bullet and the magazine away from us.

I managed to yank the gun away from him, though it was empty, and proceeded to get to my knees. He tried to do the same, so I lunged at his throat, pinning him. I raised the empty pistol above my head, preparing to beat him to death with it, when a shot fired from behind me, hitting the wall to my left. Fratley took the opportunity to jab me in the side, rolling me off of him.

Fratley reached for his cane, which had fallen a short distance from him. I tried to scramble after him, but I was too slow. He grabbed the stick and brought it down on me, towards my skull. I blocked it with the barrel of my gun. He pivoted to his knees, then pressed the cane further down with all his weight behind it.

I clenched my jaw and pushed back on him, but he was determined. A quick glance to my right revealed a small coffee cup, which had rolled towards us. With one hand on the pistol to keep the cane back, I went for the cup, snagging it with the tip of my index finger. With a strong, decisive motion, I slammed it into Fratley's jaw, knocking him sideways.

As he fell, I reached for the cane, quickly tossing it behind me. Before he could move, I leapt on top of him, straddling his chest and grabbing his collar. With all the strength I had, I decked him in the face, striking him so hard it numbed my knuckles. Blood spattered from his nose as I continued beating him like a man possessed, and after a moment his mouth dropped open, like he was about to talk.

Before he could, I slammed my bloodied fist into his cheek again.

"Jace!" called Lex from across the ship.

The sound of my name jarred me, and I stopped with my fist hovering above Fratley's head. He had a dizzying look on him, like he was lost and confused, about to black out.

"Mr. Jace!" yelled the little girl.

I dropped Fratley by the shirt and instantly rose to my feet, turning towards the back of the ship. "Lex?"

"Help!" she cried. "Mr. Jace, please help!"

I started running, snagging Fratley's cane as I bolted through the lounge and into the corridor to the airlock.

As I rounded the back corner of the ship, I saw Octavia on the floor, a man standing over her. He had my pistol in his hand, aimed at Octavia.

I threw the cane at him, hitting him in the arm. He fired the gun instantly, hitting the side of the corridor wall.

I sped up as I neared him, ramming my shoulder into his chest and knocking him back. He dropped the pistol, so I swept my hand under the gun and brought it up to meet him, letting a bullet loose right as my barrel found his stomach. It struck him true, right in his belly. He staggered, but came at me again, as though he was unaware of the injury.

I pulled the trigger again, only to hear a *click*. The pistol was empty.

The thug collided with me. He was twice my weight, and his body fell on me, knocking me to the floor. He brought both his fists up and slammed them into my chest, forcing the wind from my lungs.

I wheezed, trying to push him away.

He hit me again, and pain rattled through me. I couldn't breathe. My ribs were suddenly numb.

The ravager soldier grinned, even as blood pooled from his lips, and he lifted both his hands, ready to finish the job. His nose flared as he clenched his teeth.

My body tensed as I anticipated the final blow. There was nothing I could do to stop him. Nothing I could say, except—

The man's head jerked as an explosive noise filled the ship, pieces of his skull and brains splattering onto the side of the wall. He sat on me, a confused emptiness in his eyes, and then he fell forward, collapsing beside me with a loud thud.

Dr. Hitchens was standing four meters away from me, clutching the extendable pistol I'd dropped in the lounge, both his hands extended against his heavy belly. He looked absolutely horrified, like he couldn't believe what he'd just done.

Fuck, neither could I.

I pushed myself away from the freshly deceased body and slowly got to my feet. "Holy shit," I muttered, holding my aching chest. "Holy shit, Doc!"

"Did I...get him?"

I put my fingers over the barrel, lowering both his arms. "Easy."

He looked at me. "Where are the girls?"

"I'll get them back," I said. "Stay here while I'm gone, would you?"

"O-Okay," he said, staring at the dead man in the hall.

I wiped my forehead, then looked at Octavia. She was still motionless on the floor, but I couldn't worry about her now. Not when the others were still in danger. "Look after her. I'll be back in a minute."

He ran to his associate. "Octavia?" he whispered, taking her by the chin. "She's breathing! She's breathing."

"Stay with her and shout if you see anyone else," I said, entering the door to Fratley's shuttle, my weapon ready.

I slipped inside the airlock and into the shuttle, which was almost sizable enough to be its own ship. The interior was sufficient to walk upright in, and about two meters wide.

Piles of trash sat in the corner—beer and bags of junk food. A dozen empty seats lined both sides of the ship, with a curtain resting behind them. I limped my way to the rear of the section, keeping my pistol aimed and ready.

"Get away from me!" yelled Lex.

The girl's voice sent a flutter down my chest, and I doubled my speed.

I pushed the curtain aside, stepping into the back of the ship, and saw two men standing with Lex between them.

Abigail was also there, and back on her feet, much to my own surprise. One of the men had her by the hair, his fist around her neck. They seemed to be locked with one another.

"Jace!" shouted Abigail.

"Stay where you are!" yelled one of the men, his rifle pressed against Abigail's chest.

I dragged myself forward, aiming my gun at the one holding Lex. "You touch the kid and I'll send you straight to Hell."

"Try it and we'll kill them both!"

I took another step, keeping my aim steady.

"Do it, Jace!" yelled Abigail. "I can handle myself."

There was only one bullet left in my little extender pistol. Hardly enough for two thugs. I'd have to make the single shot count. "Get your hands off of the kid unless you want to see what your brains look like on the outside."

"This one is ours," he said, bending over Lex and taking her by the chin. "Just wait until we get her back to the—"

I fired the final bullet, hitting him in the jaw and destroying his face. He fell in front of Lex and she shrieked an ear-piercing scream.

The other man watched his friend hit the ground, a look of horror on his face. "You bastard!" he yelled, then turned to Abigail, no doubt to follow through with his threat.

But before he could regain himself, Abby took the rifle with her hands and forced it up, then wrapped her legs around his waist and twisted, forcing him to the floor and slamming her fist into his throat.

She released him and sprung up, back to her feet, and proceeded to kick him in the stomach. He gasped as each of the blows landed, helpless to stop her.

She took the rifle and hit him in the nose with the back of it, breaking his cartilage with a loud snap.

He screamed, and Abigail backed up, glancing at Lex. "Go to Jace, honey," she said, an eerie calmness in her voice. If it hadn't been for the cannon in her arms, I would've said she was being almost motherly.

"Okay," replied Lex, walking over the fallen, broken body beneath her. She trotted towards me, leaving bloody footprints in her wake.

Abigail raised the rifle to the soldier's chest. He opened his mouth to say something, but she wasn't giving him a chance. She squeezed the trigger and fired, creating a hole the size of my fist that went all the way through him.

The man fell, lifeless and empty, straight to the floor.

"Godsdamn," I said, right as Lex took my hand.

Abigail turned towards me, her face swollen and still bleeding. She looked like she shouldn't even be standing, like she might collapse at any moment. If it hadn't been for the rage in her eyes, the determination she wore, I might have told her to sit down. "Let's take care of the rest of them," she muttered, lifting the rifle across her chest.

I wasn't about to argue, not with a woman like that.

* * *

When we reentered the ship, I saw Hitchens and Octavia on their feet and against the wall. "You guys all right?" I asked, stepping through the airlock.

Both of them stared at me with wide-eyed expressions. Octavia shook her head, looking out of the corner of her eye to the other side of the hall.

At that moment, I saw a gun appear, followed by the man holding it as they walked into view. "Put the call in. Send our coordinates," said Fratley, holding his ear. He beamed a smile at me, moving the gun so the barrel was aimed in my direction.

"Shit," I muttered.

"You ain't lying," he said, shaking his head. "Should've killed me back there. You're getting stupid, Jace."

"Put the gun down and just leave, Fratley."

"And walk away from my money? I don't think so." He looked at Lex, who was standing behind my leg, holding my waist. "That little bitch is coming with me."

Abigail raised her rifle at him. "Touch the girl and you'll lose your head." She dropped her aim to target his hips. "Both of them."

He laughed. "So many threats. What a toxic environment you've constructed here, Jace. I don't think I like it."

"Then leave," I said.

"I will. Very soon, too. Just give me the freak and I'll let the rest of you go. Even the nun. How about that? You can keep your toy and I can still get paid. Win-win."

"Except I'm not giving Lex to you," I said.

"You'll do exactly that if you want to make it out of here alive."

I saw the same pistol Hitchens had used earlier resting in front of me, centimeters from the wall. He must have dropped it earlier when he went to check on Octavia. All I had to do was get to it before Fratley could get a shot off, but that was easier said than done.

If only Fratley didn't have his own weapon aimed at the

doctor.

I watched him tap the side of his ear. "This is Captain Oxanos. Prepare another boarding party. I need reinforcements."

"What's wrong, Fratley? You can't handle this on your own?" I asked.

He ignored me. "Repeat. This is Captain Oxanos. Someone answer me, godsdammit!"

I heard a click inside my ear. "Sir, I managed to block all outgoing transmissions. Captain Oxanos will be unable to contact his ship until he leaves."

I couldn't answer Siggy without drawing attention to myself, so I kept quiet, looking at both Octavia and Hitchens, and then at the extendable pistol on the floor. If I was quick, I might be able to get to it while Fratley was distracted.

Octavia seemed to track what I was thinking. She had both of her hands around Hitchens' arm. We eyed one another, and she gave me a slight nod.

Fratley snarled in frustration, unable to reach his ship. "Those idiots. I don't know what they're doing, but when I get over there, I'm going kill every last one of them." He glared at me. "Jace, I swear to the fucking gods, if you do anything stupid here, so help me, I'll kill this fat piece of shit where he stands, you hear me? Do you, Jace? Do you understand what I'm telling you? I'll plug every last one of your friends while you watch, and then I'll take that little girl with me and burn this ship where it floats. And I'll keep you alive for all of it, just so you can see—"

Octavia pulled Hitchens to the floor, suddenly, and I dove forward at the pistol. I quickly grabbed the gun, rolling on my knee in a single motion as I brought my sights to Fratley.

Before I could pull the trigger, however, Fratley fired at the two archaeologists, hitting Octavia in the middle of her back. She landed on top of Hitchens, who wrapped both his heavy arms around her, and they fell together against the floor.

At the same time, I unleashed a bullet of my own. It snagged Fratley's wrist, splitting bone and flesh.

Behind me, Abigail followed suit, firing her rifle and hitting him in the shoulder.

I ran forward, raising my gun and bringing it down across his face, knocking him in the jaw and nose.

Fratley fell, wheezing and bleeding, snot and blood rolling down his cheeks and lips. He tried to lift his pistol again, but collapsed his arm instead.

I pressed my foot to the ravager king's wrist, then aimed the barrel at his forehead, cocking my gun a final time. "Don't."

Abigail ran over and kicked the weapon from his weakened hand. Fratley's fingers wriggled on the floor like worms, trying to touch a gun that wasn't there. "Bastard," he muttered as spit and blood pooled out of his mouth.

"You should have left it alone," I said.

"Octavia needs help!" yelled Hitchens. "She's not moving!"

Abigail swung the rifle around her body so it was on her back, then ran to the doctor. "Easy," she said, pulling the woman off of him. "Octavia?"

"She needs to go to a hospital!" cried Hitchens.

"How bad is it?" I asked.

Abigail shook her head.

I stared at Octavia, an anger rising in me, and I dug my hand into Fratley's neck, squeezing as hard as I could. "Look what you did, you piece of—"

He tried to laugh, and it came out garbled.

"Shut the fuck up!" I shouted at him. I pulled my fist back and punched him again. He took the blow, but didn't stop laughing or coughing.

He tried his best to speak. "Union...coming...! You're—"

Before he could say another word, I buried the barrel of my gun into his mouth, pulling the trigger, splattering brains and blood against the floor beneath him.

I stood, stepping back from the body, and dropped the pistol at my feet.

# TWENTY

I stared down at the body of Fratley Oxanos, ravager leader and legendary former Renegade, lying motionless on my floor.

What had I just done?

He was on his way to bleeding out, no doubt about it, so I had no reason to kill him now. Fratley had already been disarmed, so the danger was gone. He was finished.

"You idiot," I whispered, staring at his motionless body.

"Jace, we have to do something here," pleaded Abigail, still holding Octavia.

I turned away from the corpse at my feet, hurrying over to the woman with the bullet in her spine. "Is she breathing?"

"Barely," said Abigail. "We need to get to a hospital."

"Sir, may I have your attention for a moment?" asked Sigmond. "I hate to interrupt but we have a situation."

"What is it now?" I asked, not bothering to hide my frustration.

"I'm detecting slipspace activity. Another rift is forming."

"Another rift? Who is it this time? What can you see?"

"It appears to be a Union cruiser, sir."

I looked at Fratley. Was this what he meant when he'd mentioned the Union?

"What are we going to do?" asked Hitchens.

"First, we're getting out of here," I said, looking at each of them. "We'll find a place to patch Octavia as soon as we're clear." I turned to the speaker. "Siggy, open a tunnel!"

"Right away, sir."

I felt the ship vibrate as we initiated our slip drive. It would only take a few seconds for the engines to prime, and then we'd be free and clear, barring any unforeseen circumstances.

"What about that ravager ship?" asked Abigail. "Won't it come after us?"

"I'll handle that. You all look after Octavia. Oh, and someone go get Freddie. Make sure he's okay."

"I'll check on him," said Abigail.

I started running for the cockpit, going as fast as I could through the ship. When I was finally in my seat, I fired up the quad cannons and took aim at the ravager ship, targeting their thrusters. They wouldn't be expecting us to fire, since Fratley was still onboard, but my ship was no match for a one-on-one fight. The safest option was to disable their engines before they had a chance to raise their shields, then get out of this system.

I was only going to have one chance at this.

"Here we go," I muttered, pulling the twin stick triggers and firing a barrage of torpedoes.

"Enemy ship is reacting," said Sigmond. "They're attempting to release their countermeasure flares."

I watched as a series of small pods dispersed from the larger ship, scattering into the space between us.

Three of the four torpedoes hit the newly-created field, but the last remaining missile continued toward the enemy ship.

It collided with the vessel, exploding in a wonderful display, shattering a chunk of their hull off of the craft, setting them adrift.

I brought up the scanner and checked their status. "Looks like we got them!"

"The tunnel is open, sir. Shall we proceed?"

"Do it!" I barked.

"Receiving a transmission," said Sigmond.

"Attention, this is General Marcus Brigham with the *UFS Galactic Dawn*, calling the vessel identified as *The Renegade Star*. Please respond. You are in violation of multiple Union laws, including the possession and theft of classified Union property. Stand down now or be prepared to face additional charges. You will not be warned a second time."

"Siggy, cut that channel and get us out of here!"

"Entering slip tunnel now," responded Sigmond.

I had no idea who Marcus Brigham was, but he could piss off. I wasn't going to fall for whatever he was selling.

We entered the tunnel right as the cruiser was leaving its own. I watched as the opening sealed behind us, and we pushed into the swirling emerald cloud of slipspace. We were back on the run now, for better or worse.

"What other orders do you have, sir?" asked the A.I.

"Put us through a few more tunnels and then find us a planet with a hospital," I told him. "And make sure it's as far away from Union space as possible."

\* \* \*

Abigail and I loaded the shuttle with the bodies of the ravagers. most were dead, but a few were still breathing, though they were unconscious. I didn't really care what happened to them after this. They deserved whatever they got.

Fratley was the last to be taken inside. I sat him down in one of the seats, my eyes lingering on him for longer than I realized.

His face was different now, all the rage and fury gone. He seemed so placid and calm, almost peaceful, so unlike himself. I wondered, briefly, if we all looked this way when we died. All our hate drained out of us. All our anger gone. Would Fratley find peace now? If the gods truly existed, would they treat him well?

A part of me hoped not. I wanted him to suffer for his crimes, for hurting Octavia and Abigail, for trying to take Lex. I wanted to tell him that dying wasn't good enough...that he deserved more.

But I couldn't. He was gone. For better or worse, he was free now, all his ambition finally lost. He was like anyone else now.

"Jace, are you ready?" asked Abigail. She was standing far

behind me at the entrance to the shuttle.

"I'm right behind you," I said, still looking at the dead man.

She stepped off the ship and went back through the airlock, leaving me alone. My eyes stayed on the former Renegade for a long moment before I finally turned away. "So long," I muttered.

\* \* \*

I waited in the lounge for Freddie to give me the news. Aside from Octavia, he was the only one of us with any medical training. Despite being injured himself, he was doing his best to take care of her.

"How is she?" I asked as Freddie came out of the hall.

"Not good," he said, removing his gloves. "I can't say for certain. I'm no doctor. We need to get her to a proper hospital."

I felt sick to my stomach, hearing the words. If I'd shot Fratley when I had the chance, when he was unconscious on the floor, this wouldn't have happened. "Siggy already has us going to a colony planet called Bellium. It has one of the best hospitals in the six systems. It'll take a few short hours."

"She's not in any serious danger right now, as far as I can tell," he assured me.

I nodded, slowly. "Thanks, Freddy."

"The good news is she's alive," he said. "I have faith in her."

"Faith," I said, quietly. "Yeah."

Freddie stood there for a second, but then quietly turned back to the hall, leaving me in silence.

I sat on the small couch, staring at the destroyed coffee pot in the corner and the tables that had been knocked over. I took the nearest one and straightened it, wiping the top with my sleeve.

The viewscreen was on, but muted, so I touched the controls to turn the sound up. It was the Union News Network, and the anchor I disliked was talking about a recent awards ceremony.

"I never liked that guy," said Abigail, standing near the hallway. She had a few bandages on her face, concealing her cuts and bruises. I was glad to hear her voice.

"Who does?" I asked.

She sat near me, crossing her legs and placing her arm over the back of the seat. "Have you seen the new warrant list?"

"Let me guess."

She nodded. "We're all there."

"Perfect."

She took a small pad from her right pocket and tossed it to me. "You, me, Freddie, Hitchens. We're all wanted. Two hundred thousand credits each."

I read over the document, scoffing. "A million for the whole lot of us. That's big money. We'll have every Renegade in the galaxy after us."

"Are you going to turn everyone in?" she asked.

"I'm considering it," I said, a wry smile on my face.

Abigail smiled, but it soon faded, and her eyes trailed off, focusing briefly on the television. "We can't go back now. We're done."

"It's not like either of us had anywhere to go back to in the first place," I said.

She nodded. "Not after what happened to Arcadia."

"I'm sorry about that," I muttered. "The only reason Fratley did that was because of me. I—"

I felt her hand touch mine, and my eyes lifted to see hers. "You saved us all, Jace. Forget the rest. If it wasn't for you, we'd all be dead."

I didn't say anything.

"You know," she continued. "Maybe we can find a nice beach somewhere, far from all the noise."

"A beach?" I asked, trying to imagine myself with sand between my toes.

"You never know," she said, smiling, and for the first time since I'd met her, she had a warmth to her. It made me smile.

You could open a bar," I suggested.

She scrunched her nose. "I'm no good at mixing drinks."

"Oh, right. You're a nun. I almost forgot."

"I think we both know I was never really a nun, Jace."

I nodded. "I always knew that. Somehow."

"What are you two doing?" asked Hitchens, entering the lounge from Octavia's room. Abby's hand slipped off mine as soon as the doctor spoke.

"We're just talking about what kind of alcohol to sell in our new bar," I answered.

"We're discussing our next option," corrected Abigail. "The Union has warrants on every last one of us, which means we can't go back."

"Why would you want to do a thing like that?" asked the archaeologist.

"You have a better idea, Professor?" I asked.

"If you can't return, why not press forward? We have the map to Earth. As far as I'm concerned, there's no reason not to follow it."

Abigail looked at me. "That *was* the initial plan."

"Except it didn't include me," I added.

"That was then," she said.

"We could use your expertise, Captain," said Hitchens.

"That map has you leaving the Deadlands," I said. "My so-called expertise only extends so far. I've never been beyond this part of space. I don't know what's out there."

"Not many do," said Hitchens.

I shook my head. "What about Octavia?"

"I've spent the last seven years with her at my side. I know she wants nothing more than to see this mission through to the end. Since I met her, it's been her dream, and mine."

I had to admit, the idea of seeing the unknown was enticing. There were plenty of colonies beyond the Deadlands. Plenty of worlds with people on them. A few other empires, such as the Sarkonians, who kept to themselves. I'd always wanted to see their worlds. This could be my chance.

At the same time, I knew I couldn't go home again, not after everything I'd done. Taurus Station wouldn't have me now...and Ollie was gone.

Aside from these people, who else did I really have? Where else could I go?

"How about it, Jace?" asked Abigail.

I looked at both of them. Hitchens with his belly and jovial mustache, still smiling at me, even despite Octavia's situation. Abigail with her quiet resolve, determined to fulfill her mission.

And Lex, standing at the doorway, there in the corner of the lounge, watching me with that strange, intense curiosity. I played like I hadn't seen her there, but I knew she was waiting to hear my answer.

"Okay," I finally said, looking back at Abigail. "I'll take you where you want to go. I'll help you find your way to Earth, wherever it is."

She smiled. We all did.

"Wonderful!" exclaimed the archaeologist, coming to my side. He reached his hand out, and I took it. He pulled me on my feet and wrapped his arms around me. "This is a true gift, Captain. Thank you!"

"Easy," I said, pushing him off. "Personal space."

"This should be an interesting trip," said Abigail.

"Think so?" I asked.

"If the last few days are any indication," she said.

"Let's plot a course, then," I said, cracking my knuckles. "First Bellium, and then to Earth."

"To Earth," agreed Hitchens.

"Wherever it is," said Abigail.

I placed a hand on both their shoulders. "Here's hoping it really does exist."

# EPILOGUE

I sat in the cockpit, staring at the little box Hitchens had given me. It was a piece of ancient technology, a kind of holographic storage device.

A tiny, porcelain finger reached out and touched the top of the cube, and it caused a series of lights to illuminate before me, showing the next coordinates.

I turned to see the little girl, Lex, sitting beside me, smiling a wide grin. She had a toy rocket in her hand, the same one I'd seen her playing with the other day. "Like that?" she asked.

"Exactly like that," I answered.

She slapped her knees. "Where are we going now?"

"Looks like..." I paused, staring at the display. "Somewhere in Sector 2210. Siggy, you got that?"

"I am already charting a course, sir," replied the A.I.

"See there? You did it, kid," I told Lex.

"Will I get sit up here with you from now on?" she asked.

"Normally, I wouldn't allow anyone in here with me," I said.

She started to frown.

I raised my finger. "For you, kid, we'll make an exception."

"Really?" she asked, widening her eyes.

"We're partners, right?" I asked.

She furrowed her brow, very seriously. "Partners," she said, nodding.

"Slip drive is ready. Awaiting your orders, sir," said Siggy.

I looked at Lex. "You want to give the order?"

She grinned, eagerly. "Really? But I'm not the captain."

"This will be an exception," I said. "Think you can handle it?"

She nodded, still smiling. "Okay. Okay, I've got it!"

"Let's hear it, kid."

The little albino girl gripped the sides of her chair, and with the most commanding voice I'd ever heard from her, she said, "Punch it, Siggy!"

# AUTHOR NOTES

Hey there! I hope you're enjoying *The Renegade Star* series so far. It's a completely different kind of story than what I'm used to writing, but it's something I've wanted to do for a while. I grew up watching a lot of space westerns as a kid (Cowboy Bebop, Trigun, etc.), so I've always had a deep love for that kind of story.

The great thing about scifi is that you can explore new ideas and unique settings, while still having characters that feel relatable. I'll be doing plenty of that in this series, as our heroes traverse the unknown regions of the galaxy in search of Earth and all its many secrets. Of course, we'll also learn about Lex and her mysterious origins, but hey, all in good time.

With my last series, *The Variant Saga*, it took me several months to write each entry (the second book took nearly 10 months!). That was a bit too slow for my tastes, so this time I'll be aiming for a book every 4-6 *weeks*. It's going to be a personal challenge for me, but with your help, I'm sure I can do it. I'm having such a blast with this story and I plan to keep it that way.

Until next time, keep sailing, Renegades,

*J.N. Chaney*

# ABOUT THE AUTHOR

J. N. Chaney has a Master's of Fine Arts in creative writing and fancies himself quite the Super Mario Bros. fan. When he isn't writing or gaming, you can find him online at www.jnchaney.com.

He migrates often but was last seen in Avon Park, Florida. Any sightings should be reported, as they are rare.

*Renegade Star* is his sixth novel.

11356070R00150

Printed in Great Britain
by Amazon